Recipe For Romance by Maria Isabel Pita

Recipe For Romance is both erotic and romantic. Freelance journalist Ariana Padron goes home to Miami for a funeral, never expecting to meet her soul mate, Gerald, a talented sculptor. Love hits hard and fast, and so does passion. The story is laced with very steamy sex, the colors and textures of good food, and much discussion of love. Highly sensual, this author has a talent for rich description. I definitely recommend this story if you like your romance smoking hot. *Just Erotic Romance Reviews*

Mutual Holdings by Susan DiPlacido

Ms. DiPlacido is a thoroughly seasoned author, and it shines through with this outstandingly written book. Ms. DiPlacido lets Lisa do the talking, and what a talker Lisa is. She relates her tale of confused and frustrated love, leaving the reader in stitches. Lisa's dry humor is biting at times. You will come away from this story feeling like a friendship has developed, the closeness only a good writer can achieve and deliver to its fullest degree. The only thing you might not like about this book is your inability to put it down. *Road to Romance*

Whispered Secrets by Terri Pray

I thoroughly enjoyed reading Whispered Secrets with such an independent and confident heroine who knows what she wants out of life, and in her bedroom. Ms. Pray does an excellent job of keeping the momentum of the story alive without boring her readers. Whispered Secrets touches on some modern day dating dilemmas and the issues single women face in relationships. The characters are... real people you can associate with; especially seeing them grow as individuals through the love, trust and faith they discover in each other. This contemporary tale of the love Kate unexpectedly discovers with Frank is gratifying and ends on a high note. I would recommend Whispered Secrets for anyone who is interested in contemporary erotic romance.   *Just Erotic Romance Reviews*

Cat's Collar by Maria Isabel Pita

What makes this novel great is what it isn't, that is, much of today's erotica has had to sell itself on extreme BDSM and violence against women that makes the ordinary person cringe. Ms. Pita manages to take us on an erotic journey with Mira and Phillip as they explore each other both physically and mentally to discover that perhaps there is such a thing as a soul mate. Not only the gentle side of love but also the hot sizzling sex scenes in the book are written with superb skill.   *Rudolf Spoerer*

First Magic Carpet Books, Inc. edition March 2006

Published in 2006

Manufactured in the United States of America
Published by Magic Carpet Books, Inc.

Magic Carpet Books, Inc.
PO Box 473
New Milford, CT 06776

ISBN: 0977431118

Book Design: P. Ruggieri

A Brush
With Love

by Maria Isabel Pita

Author's Note

**None of the feelings expressed
in this book are fiction.**

Chapter One

When the wind isn't blowing, Miranda can enjoy the penetrating cold. Rather than feeling lost in all the layers composing her, she feels more centered than ever in the warm core of her self. The vital little organ of her ipod resting safely in a pocket over her heart, her long legs taking her briskly up-and-down streets that all somehow lead to home, she is pleasingly aware of all the parts of her, not just those that can be seen.

Knee-high black leather boots she has owned for years tightly hug her calves, doubly protected by black flannel leggings that flow up to her slender thighs, and cradle her pussy in a breathable white triangle of cloth pressing against the even luckier material of her cotton panties. She always remembers what color she's wearing, and this evening it's blue turquoise, the fabric moist and warm as the Caribbean sea they resemble clinging to the lips of her labia, shaved smooth as a rosy pink seashell but infinitely softer than sand.

Her slender but curvaceous hips (one of the things that got her the job) gyrate with all the smooth efficiency of youth beneath a tight black wool skirt that barely brushes the tops of her boots. During the winter, there's always a fine cotton T-shirt clinging to her torso, and to the nipples crowning her pert round breasts, another natural gift helping her pay the rent.

The animal-soft burgundy-colored cashmere sweater feels more luxuriously sensual against her flesh the colder it gets. Then there's the black wool scarf wrapped tightly three times around her neck, because if the mysterious column between her body and her brain is cold none of her is warm. The tips of her ears, her hands and her feet are very sensitive, so she has an extra pair of socks on over her tights, a black hat contains her long auburn hair, and insulated tight black leather gloves protect her fingers while still enabling her to operate her ipod.

Of course, no one who passes her on the street can see much of her except the ankle-length black coat made in Romania she was lucky enough to find at a thrift store. If it could keep some inhabitant of the Carpathian mountains warm, ancient and mythical land of vampires, it's certainly enough protection for her young Boston bones, and its numerous secret pockets free her from the burden of a purse. Her full lips, gently smiling as she savors the sense of herself, are also protected by an invisible layer of aloe Vera lip gloss with spf-15 like the facial cream she applies every morning to keep her skin soft and pliant in the frigid temperatures; the natural botanical components protecting her from the chaffing cold and the withering gusts of central heat.

It's a long walk from the train station to her apartment; every evening Miranda has time to take youthfully smug inventory of her self which only begins with the superficial layers of her clothing, because then there's her skin, that vulnerably exposed organ that needs so much help keeping warm, and the muscles beneath it, the look and flow of which she is more familiar with than most young women, although the stark black charcoal sketches and hasty pastels don't do justice to the vivid red power of her ligaments clinging to bones the color of artists' paper. She imagines her skeleton has the slightly rough smoothness of a blank canvas on which the artist of her soul created her colorfully unique appearance.

But there's more to her even than the soft purses of her organs containing the priceless treasure of her life. Her lungs – silently protesting the freezing air animating their tender bud-like sacks – her heart beating in rhythm with her stride, her stomach rumbling gently because she's hungry, none of these parts of herself are the ones thinking about them while listening to music flowing from her headset; little black plastic organs inserted into the spiraling shells of her ears pumping the pounding rhythm of one song after another into her bloodstream, some crashingly loud and angry, others gentle and hauntingly beautiful as a low tide at sunset.

The streets of Arlington, Massachusetts are as familiar to Miranda as the sight of her own written name, yet she never feels, and they never look, exactly the same. As she turns onto her block, the usual windows are lit up, yet the mood of the light glowing from inside is always subtly affected by her own. If she's sad for some reason, the black wrought iron lamps curving over the street look like people with their heads bent in sadness, and she is aware mostly of the dark spaces in the apartment buildings around her. But on this evening as on most others, being so intensely aware of the different parts of herself is invigorating, and fills her with a much deeper and positive hope than can be generated by the endorphins activated by her brisk pace all the way from the station to her doorstep. She looks up at individual windows as she walks, Bono's voice reverberating in her skull superimposing images of Africa and painfully thin children dying of AIDS against luminous window panes promising all the comforts possible on earth. When she's walking out on the streets at night, in the freezing cold, people's warmly lit homes seem so much more than just doors leading onto wooden floors or carpeted rooms and televisions perennially flickering like water illuminated by a restless power source that never sets.

As she cups her gloved hands in front of her face and blows to feel the warmth of her breath against her achingly cold cheeks, her eyes rise to her own dark third story window and she suffers the thrill of wondering who he is, *where* he is, the man who will truly turn her on and enable her to step into that other dimension where her home is not just a cold apartment with an astronomical heating bill, but a golden world where everything is possible.

It's impossible to be bored if you really notice everything. It seems to Miranda that anyone who suffers from boredom must be living in a sensory void. Just coming home from work in the evening constitutes an explosion of sensations that fills her with a very real happiness, even if she is lonely and expectantly waiting even deeper fulfillments. As she hurries up the front steps, she switches off her ipod so she can enjoy the sound of her heels clicking confidently on the stone. By now she already has her keys in hand, and they toll a quiet satisfaction as she thrusts the most important one into the lock, and with a satisfied cluck lets herself in to the old building.

It isn't much warmer in the lobby, and two of the three overhead lights in the narrow corridor are burned out and will most likely remain that way for weeks, if not months, making it hard to see the faded numbers on the metal mailboxes, twelve of them. She quickly inserts the smallest key into number nine, as usual her hope spiking at the possibility she has received something interesting, but of course it's usually just junk mail, or worse, another bill. In contrast a magazine feels like a gift, and a loving letter from her mom is always a soothing balm to impersonal advertisements. Tonight she finds a wonderfully fat issue of *Cooking Light*, and one of those cards printed in blue-and-white with the vague faces of two lost souls last seen a hopelessly long time ago. The feel of the crisp plastic around the magazine clutched in her leather gloved fingers is for some reason a gratifying sensation without actually being one. The seeds of the recipes she's holding in her hand are all warm and fragrant, a promisingly powerful contrast to the cold stale lobby. Arriving home means the end of another day and all interesting possibilities, yet it also feels deliciously full of promise.

Her boots make a more subdued sound on the carpeted stairway, worn wooden steps winding up to the third floor and her apartment at the end of the hall. Once inside, she locks the door behind her, sets her keys on a small table along with the magazine, and yanks out her earphones to better appreciate the quality of the silence that greets her. Intense quiet is a sensation in itself, and despite the cold, she always leaves her curtains open all day because she loves the atmosphere of her living room illuminated only by street light. For an instant she feels like the interesting and beautiful heroine of a nineteen-forties film noir movie where there is only the black-and-white of profound shadows defined by light, the haunting set of the drama of her life. Then the snap of a lamp turning on and the whole scene changes into one of colorful eclectic comfort.

She switches on the heat, unconsciously smiling at her things, which always wait patiently for her to return to the simple pleasures they so unselfishly give her. Then the gloves come off and she becomes wonderfully conscious of textures again. The wool of her Romanian coat feels slightly rough (she likes to think of it as her big black sheep) and she thanks it for protecting her as she hangs it up on the antique coat rack she found at yet another one of favorite thrift stores. It always feels so nice to take off her hat and sense the electric crackle of her hair wafting up into the air, her skull enjoying the cool freedom after its warm confinement.

It is so cold in her apartment an icy hand might as well be wrapping frigid fingers around her neck as she unwinds her scarf, and hangs it up next to her coat and hat. Not a pillow is out of place; she always leaves everything in perfect order so she can truly savor coming home. Once she didn't have time to make her bed, and the sight of empty cold rumpled sheets ineffably depressed her. She makes sure not to let it happen again. Her body is only twenty-three, but deep inside she has somehow always felt ages old. Her mother is worried that her only daughter is lonely living by herself, but the rooms of her apartment as she walks through them are blessed by the absence of a potentially noisy, overly talkative, all-to-normal roommate. Miranda is too neat, too sensitive, to introspective, too everything to endure living with a stranger. How she can afford nine-hundred square feet of space with polished wooden floors and elegant crown molding all by herself is not a question with a reasonable answer. It simply, miraculously, is, and it feels absolutely right even though she never could have made it happen if she actually tried. Her landlady looks a thousand years old, and she regularly raises the rent of all her other tenants while keeping Miranda's as low as it has been for three years since she moved in.

She walks into her dark bedroom, and pauses. If she doesn't turn on a light, she can imagine she is not alone, that from the impenetrable shadows a man is watching her as she pulls off her sweater. This man is not a thief or a rapist, he has not entered her apartment through the front door; his black jacket and pants are part of the darkness itself, a reflection of streetlight in her mirror an evanescent glint of eyes that can see into her soul. He knows how much she longs for his touch, for his kisses and his thrusts. She tosses her sweater onto a chair. Her nipples are so hard they almost hurt, and she can't slip out of her skirt fast enough. She sits on the edge of the bed, relishing the softness of her feather comforter after the hard plastic seat of the train and hours on her feet. She slips off her boots, and then quickly peels off her tights, leaving on her white cotton t-shirt and turquoise panties as she lies back against her feather pillows.

The way the intense cold inhabiting her cozy bedroom possesses her makes her tremble as if she's excited. Not an inch of her flesh can escape the terribly stimulating caress. The sound of the old heaters clicking on through the apartment as they slowly fill with hot water cannot compare to the excitement that swiftly rises inside her at the sight and feel of her highly desirable young body. She is a little frightened, there actually could be a man standing somewhere in the darkness watching her as she clutches one of her breasts through the fine cotton and slips a hand into her panties.

God she loves the sensation of the silky-soft flesh cushioning her beautifully shaped bones. Her pussy is a miracle of moist warmth to her dry cold fingertips, a tropical garden of carnivorous petals engulfing two of her digits as she swiftly slides them up inside her, deliberately not preparing herself, letting the man in the shadows penetrate her without a word, without a softening kiss or endearment. The sound of her helpless gasp arouses her even further. She lets go of herself to yank off her T-shirt, then falls back against the pillows again to admire the sight of her lovely round breasts, her nipples reaching for the ceiling turning her on with how hard and yet how exquisitely vulnerable they are. She keeps her panties on to tease herself, the soft cotton caressing her labia as she concentrates three fingertips on her clitoris. She presses down and moves them around and around as she spreads her legs as far as she can, opening herself up to the spirit of the man haunting the room and possessing her. She splays herself open as she pretends it isn't her hand squeezing her young breasts, then pinching and pulling on her nipples, then reaching up to clutch her throat so she can't cry out, so she has to struggle to breathe even as an orgasm crests effortlessly between her legs; crashing through her pelvis with such energy her back arches and her legs come together trying to control the devastating force of the ecstasy.

Now the room is empty. She can reach over and turn on the bedside lamp and see, if not really believe, she is alone. He *had* been there, whoever he was, he *is* here with her; her imagination is simply a way of seeing him that bypasses her reason and her physical senses. She is relaxed now, she can wait another day, and another day after that if she has to, to meet him, at the moment she can be happy with a long hot shower, and a glass of wine she'll sip as she listens to NPR while preparing dinner.

Chapter Two

The oil truck pulled up outside Miranda's building. Not everyone was home from work yet. Patrick was able to wedge himself between two cars, now he didn't have to worry about being double parked and blocking traffic if he lingered. This was his last stop for the evening, it always was, even if he had to go out of his way. He was filling two tanks tonight, apartment three and apartment nine.

He opened the truck door and leapt out onto the street with all the energy of an expectation he fully expected to be frustrated, but he was still looking forward to seeing her. She *had* to be home, if she wasn't, he would be tempted to leave and come back tomorrow, to hell with the mileage. But he wasn't too worried; she was usually there. It was hard to believe such a beautiful girl wasn't taken yet. The young men these days ought to have their heads examined, he thought, letting a creature like that escape their grasp.

He ran up the steps and rang the buzzer for apartment three. He had been working this job for over twenty years, and more than once he had found himself tempted to cheat on his wife, but it was always a passing, easily resisted, fantasy. It was very different with the girl in apartment nine. For nearly three years she had not been out of his mind, although at first he only thought about her on the days he saw her name and address on his manifest. Lately, however, he was increasingly obsessed with her, to the point where he always scheduled her delivery for last even if he had to go out of his way.

The tenant in number three quickly buzzed him into the building. It was December in Boston and Patrick literally helped keep everyone alive. Swiftly and lithely for a man in his late forties, his heavy boots tolling on the concrete basement steps, he went efficiently about his business wondering if she could hear the sound of his hose pumping the vital fluid into her tank. The engine made a loud noise; unless she was listening to music or in the shower, by now she was expecting his quiet knock on her door.

Patrick barely noticed the Oriental man who opened the door of number three and signed a good portion of his paycheck away to him. He was wondering what he could say to her that might win him the seemingly impossible prize of an invitation into her apartment. If this was another century, she might ask him in for a cup of hot tea to warm him up, but in the comfortable new millennium people took care of themselves and gorgeous young college girls didn't socialize with middle-aged blue collar workers. Or did they? He wasn't sure *what* young people did besides talk on cell phones all day. He didn't even know if she *was* in college, only that she was young and intelligent enough to be, he could tell she was by the intent manner in which she looked at him as she smiled. He had told himself over and over again that her expression had nothing to do with him, that she was simply being polite, but lately a part of him was less inclined to listen to reason and more tempted to hope.

Finally on the third floor, he paused in front of her door to smooth back his wind disheveled dark-blonde hair. Thank God he wasn't showing any signs whatsoever of going gray or bald, and he still had broad shoulders and strong arms even if all they had the pleasure of holding these days was a seven-year-old child. His other two kids had already left home, and once they were alone again, his wife's interest in sex had resurrected just long enough for her to become pregnant again. They still slept in the same bed, but that was all either one of them had the energy or desire to do, at least with each other. He was wearing a knee-length black leather coat over his black uniform. He knew he looked good. He was six-feet-two, and even though time and bitter weather had scored a few laughter lines around his eyes and mouth, he was still a handsome man, of that he had no doubt. He knocked firmly on the door three times.

"Just a minute!" her voice called from inside.

He waited, trying not to hold his breath; trying to look relaxed, not excited to be there.

The door opened. "Hi, Patrick," she said, smiling, but for some reason more hesitantly than normal.

"Hi, Miranda." He had never seen her in a black bathrobe. His already expectantly firm cock hardened a few more degrees realizing she had just hastily wrapped the thick cotton around her naked body. The faintly perfumed scent of her slightly damp, warm skin was such a contrast to the freezing night outside he almost felt intoxicated by it as he held the clipboard out towards her mutely. She was so incredibly beautiful he could think of nothing to say.

She reached for the pen resting securely beneath the clip, just as he belatedly made to pull it out himself and save her the trouble. His large fingers landed over her slender ones, and the feel of her skin sent an electric shock through him he realized an instant later had been real as she gasped, and pulled her hand away.

"Wow…" Her smile dimmed, and she made sure their fingers didn't touch again as she accepted the pen from him, and signed her name with her usual confident flourish.

"Well, I guess that's it," he declared lamely, his eyes staring intently into hers as he desperately tried to think of some excuse to linger on her doorstep. "This is my last stop for the night."

"It really is very cold out," she remarked slowly, as if it meant something. Her gaze broke shyly away from his, taking in his strong, tall body. "I hope you don't have a terribly long drive home." She sounded absolutely sincere as she raised her eyes to his again.

"It's pretty long." He could just make out the gentle swell of her delicate cleavage between the folds of her robe.

"Where do you live?"

"Dorchester." Was it wishful thinking on his part or was she deliberately making conversation? Either way he was glad to still be there.

"That *is* pretty far," she agreed. "I hope the traffic's not *too* bad."

He shrugged. "I'm in no rush." He held her eyes, the clipboard forgotten at his side. She hadn't washed her hair and it looked lovelier than ever against her black robe.

"Would you like something hot to drink before you head back?" she said abruptly. "I mean, since you're not in a rush." She sounded uncertain, as if he might actually refuse her offer, or as if she couldn't quite believe she had made it.

"I would like that, thank you." He stepped into the apartment, careful not to brush against her as he did so.

"All I have is tea." She closed the door behind him slowly, as if regretting her offer and trying to find a gracious way out of it. "I don't drink coffee."

He set his clipboard down on the table beside them. "I can do without the tea, Miranda," he confessed quietly.

She glanced down at his free hands as if in alarm. The clipboard had always been between them, but now it was gone and a man she didn't really know at all had crossed the threshold into her home where she stood naked beneath her robe. He saw these thoughts flash in her eyes, and understood that neither one of them could possibly pretend there was a respectable excuse for his presence. He was over twenty years older than she was, and married. He knew nothing about her, and she knew even less about him, yet she had invited him in, and the excuse of a hot drink was a flimsy bandage over the desire flowing between them. It was there, he could feel it's vital heat as clearly as he could see her looking up at his face waiting for him to tell her what he preferred instead of tea.

He urged her back against the door by stepping towards her, using her body to block his way out so she knew there was no turning back now. Her eyes widened as her lips parted, but it was more surprise at his boldness he saw reflected back at him in her dark-green irises than fear. Grasping her upper arms, he bent and pressed his mouth hard against hers. Holding her firmly, he thrust his tongue between her lips and kissed her like the starving man he was. He only released her long enough to reach down for the belt of her robe. He undid the simple knot with two impatient tugs, savoring the flavor of her moan as it rose up from deep in her body through her throat and into their joined mouths. He could scarcely believe she was kissing him back, but the sounds she was making were definitely not ones of protest. He had never heard a more beautiful music in all his life than her deep, helpless, submissive moans. He answered them with a gratefully gentle yet deeply determined groan of his own as he clutched her breasts hungrily in both hands. He couldn't remember anything ever feeling as good as her soft little tits did to him then, and the way her nipples immediately hardened, digging into the coarse heart of his palms, acted like mysterious buttons triggering the certainty inside him that he could have her if he dared.

Keeping one of her breasts captive, he caressed the tender flesh of her belly, moving cautiously, hopefully down towards her pussy. He pulled out of their passionate kiss and whispered, "God, you're beautiful!" just as he forcefully cradled her cunt in his hand. He couldn't believe it, not just that he had a very real piece of heaven warming up his fingers, but that she was smooth and pure and flawless to the touch like the sacred shrine she was to his painfully buried cock. He suffered the impression then that his whole life might have been different if his wife had ever cared enough to shave her sex for him.

"Oh, no!" she breathed, but she wasn't looking beseechingly up into his eyes appealing to his higher senses, she was gazing down at his hand, and there was something about her expression – slightly frightened yet so avidly expectant – that transported him beyond the few cautious thoughts the growing size of his erection left room for. He was suddenly filled to bursting with faith, not in some senseless God but in himself, in every virile fiber of his being, because he could feel – he was holding the evidence in his hand – that she wasn't merely tolerating his advances; she wanted him, she *wanted* him to fuck her.

He was so much bigger than she was that her entire tender vulva rested against his hard palm, her labial lips giving his life-line a moist kiss full of promise for the immediate, tangible future and to hell with everything else. He stroked her, digging the heel of his hand into the tender crown of her mons where her clitoris was. He couldn't feel it, but he could see it as she gasped and looked up into his eyes that his caress was giving her pleasure.

Maria Isabel Pita

"Do you like that?" he asked gruffly, suddenly angry as he wondered how many men she had looked up at like this.

"Yes…" Her arms remained passive at her sides, her hands pressed against the door as if she needed to brace herself to endure the intense sensations he was forcing on her.

Groaning again in something like pain at how long these moments had taken to become real, he brought his ravenous mouth down over her exposed breast, and the way she cried out enhanced the delightful taste of her nipple, at once so stiff and yielding, caught between his lips. Her pussy in one hand, one of her breasts squeezed possessively in the other, his mouth full of her other mound's luscious tenderness, he rubbed her clit with his working man's rough hand until she moaned, and moaned again, and then again more and more breathlessly, a whimpering, pleading note entering her voice. Her nipples were so hard they literally felt like seeds as he sensed pleasure blooming inexorably through her body.

He let go of her abruptly, spun her around, and pulled off her robe, letting it fall to the floor. For a wild moment he considered fucking her from behind right there and then. He visualized ramming his rampant cock into her tight little pussy from behind, but he had enough control left to realize that would upset her.

"Come on." He took her hand and led her into the bedroom. Doing it on the bed was more normal, less impersonal, softer; she could pretend he had some tender feelings for her.

"Patrick, no, please, I can't…"

He cursed himself for giving her a fatally long minute to think about it. He didn't reply. If he indulged her doubts with even a single word now, all was lost. Instead he let his best worst instincts kick in and said, "Get on the bed." He flung off his coat and yanked his zipper down. "On your hands and

23

knees," he added in a commanding tone, wresting his erection out of his pants through the slit in his underwear, and his dick pulsed triumphantly in his hand as, unbelievably, she obeyed him, crawling cat-like onto the mattress.

Without even taking off his boots, he knelt on the bed behind her. She had glimpsed the size of his cock before she turned around, she knew what she had coming to her, and by God he was going to *give* it to her.

He found himself pressing a hand against her upper back and gently but firmly forcing her facedown into a pillow. "Like that." His voice was a hoarse growl. He yanked her hips up with both hands, his eyes devouring the vision of the rosy temple doors he could scarcely believe were granting him entry. She made a small, mewing sound, bracing herself for his thrust. He paused, unable to believe the extent of his luck, momentarily lost in the gleaming fall of her hair down her back, the dip of her spine where it flowed into her ass absolutely the sexiest and the sweetest thing he had ever seen. Holding the cock he had not been so proud of in years, he stroked the sweetly crinkled flesh of her vulva up and down with the engorged head of his erection, watching her labial lips bloom open around him. He was so hard that the sensation dissolved his intention to exercise control. Instead of penetrating her slowly and gratefully and making an effort to stoke her excitement along with his, he dug his rough fingers into her tender skin, and nearly lifting her off the bed slipped her pussy on like a glove made just for him.

He couldn't quite bring himself to care, but he didn't think he was hurting her, she was too slick and warm and accommodating to every last inch of his hard-on as he drove into her. If sinning by cheating on his wife and giving in to his basest desires could feel this good, he would gladly buy the ticket to hell himself as long as the burning lust that had tormented him could just once in a hundred years be assuaged by the divinely soothing dimension of this beautiful pussy.

"Oh, Patrick… oh, my God!"

He breathless vulnerability coupled with her absolute submission to his pounding rhythm was too much for him. He penetrated her over and over again with all his strength, with every vindicated ounce of energy he possessed, and the longer she just lay there taking it, not moving a muscle to resist him, the more he couldn't believe it and the crazier it made him. His fingers dug relentlessly into her tender hips as he pounded his pulsing dick into her faster and harder, how earnestly her innermost flesh embraced his rending length encouraging his violence. When he came, he was only vaguely ashamed of the amount of sperm he was pumping into her, what remained of his reason half expecting his pent up explosion of cum to scald her tender young insides.

Chapter Three

The man who had hired Miranda for the day greeted her civilly. He walked her over to where she could hang her coat and scarf and hat, then just watched as she divested herself without offering to help, but then of course he was a Harvard professor with more important things to think about than behaving like a gentleman. "Where's your purse?" he said almost accusingly, as if she was deliberately planning to blame his department for the loss.

"I don't have one. I carry everything around in my pockets."

"I see." He did seem to have to make an effort to focus on her as a person through all the much more important tasks crowding his tenured brain. "I'm afraid we can only turn the thermostat up so high." His boyishly large dark-brown eyes looked inexpressibly sad, or profoundly bored, it was hard to tell probably because he wasn't sure himself. "I can't have my class falling asleep," he explained why it was necessary for her to suffer.

"Oh, that's all right," she assured him blithely. "I'm used to it."

"You work as an artist's model at Mass Art?"

"Yes, sir." She glanced shyly over her shoulder. Students were beginning to enter the room, stacks of textbooks cradled in their arms like the dismantled stones of an ancient temple, ponderously heavy and strangely depressing now that they were no longer part of a sacred whole.

"Well, um…"

"Miranda."

"Well, Miranda, we'll be ready to start soon."

"Great."

His hands abruptly thrust themselves into the pockets of his crumpled khaki slacks almost as if he felt guilty about what they were going to do to her. "This will be a little different than posing for artists, Miranda."

"Yes, I know." He was a relatively handsome older man, and right now the last thing she wanted to think about, or be around, were handsome older men. She still couldn't believe what she had done last night.

"You can sit here." He indicated an uncomfortable-looking wooden chair. "I'll call you when we're ready."

"Okay." She tugged her gray wool skirt down primly over her knees and seated herself like a little girl punished into a corner for being so thrillingly wicked. Yet just because she had let a man who was essentially a complete stranger to her (not to mention married) fuck her last night didn't mean she was a bad person. Patrick was the one who should be feeling guilty today, yet she fervently hoped he wasn't. She wanted him to know that the way he had fucked her felt so good, body and soul she was still enjoying a mindless afterglow that had kept her warm all night and all morning, and looked as if it was going to carry her through the rest of the day into the evening.

She forced herself out of bed early, deliciously dazed, afraid of being late. She made it to the Harvard campus in good time, but once there she got hopelessly lost in a maze of red-brick buildings surrounded by equally old and venerable trees, their ink-black limbs a judgmental cursive against the white sky spelling out what a common, loose young woman she was, along with every other insult her shocked self-esteem could think of. She had to ask at least four people for directions before she finally found the right set of stone steps. She shoved open the door leading into the building with her whole body, and at long last central heat engulfed her like the spirit of a loving relative she had missed painfully. That morning she had *not* been enjoying the cold. How confused she was by her behavior last night gave the freezing wind the power to cut into her with self-doubts that made her eyes tear up miserably.

She was sitting partially hidden behind the classroom door. Most of the students as they filed in – some in chatting groups of two or more, most somberly alone – didn't notice her. Miranda sat with her long legs crossed and her hands clasped as if in prayer. She was interested in the students who were alert enough to look around them and notice her behind the door; the ones who weren't completely wrapped up in the numbing cocoon of their lofty futures and still managed to see the world around them and, ideally, all the sensual delights of the present. She was a little nervous, she had never done this before, and the fact that most of the students were most likely intelligent and wealthy young men didn't help her relax. She was always on the look out for her soul mate, and for weeks, ever since she accepted this assignment, she had been fantasizing about meeting him here. Any circumstance was as good as another for Fate, but this one had seemed especially promising because it was on a different campus than the one she worked at every day. She had not planned on fucking a total stranger the night before, however, and now somehow everything felt mysteriously short-circuited, as if, at least for the moment, she had hopelessly damaged the mysterious web of her destiny. She no longer felt there was any chance the man she was destined to meet and love would be here today, which made her furious because, naturally, she knew it was her Catholic upbringing enforcing a period of penance on her for being such a bad girl and daring to have sex with a man she didn't love and who didn't love her, and who was, worst of all, married. Therefore, subconsciously, she was suffering the punishment of feeling cut off from the magic pattern of her destiny. Yet the truth was that she was still subliminally purring from how hard, how roughly and how selfishly – from how totally wonderfully – he had fucked her.

By the time the professor walked over and closed the door leading out into the hallway, Miranda had determined her soul mate was indeed not present that day. She had studied every young man who walked in, and not one of them struck a cord of recognition inside her that rang back through the ages and all her past lives and forward into all her future incarnations. She was relieved. The memory of Patrick's erection pulsing deep inside her as he climaxed was still too fresh and intense for her to keep thinking profound thoughts about destiny or anything else.

"Miranda, we're ready to begin."

She quickly got up and walked over to the professor where he stood by the side of his big desk, in front of an old-fashioned blackboard, facing the class. The attention of each student was costing someone an unholy amount of money, so it was seriously silent in the room to the point of church-like reverence. At once she fell into the technique she had developed of turning her vision inward so all the faces before her became featureless blurs powerless to affect her in any way. She was centered in herself, and for hours all her movements – most importantly the absolute stillness she was paid for – would stem from this inner core filled with a boundless, peaceful grace. Her hands were perfectly steady, her face expressionless and composed as she grasped the bottom of her black turtleneck sweater with both hands, and pulled it off over her head in one smooth gesture. She wasn't wearing anything beneath it. She focused on an empty desk at the back of the room. She didn't need to see the faces of the pre-Med students observing her to sense how they studiously avoided showing any reaction whatsoever to the sight of her bare breasts. It amused her to think that the first mental note they made in class that day was that she definitely didn't have implants. Patrick had obviously liked her pert all-natural tits, he couldn't seem to get enough of them, and she had been thrilled by the way his hands completely engulfed them, and by the rough way he squeezed and kneaded them. An irresistible warmth awoke between her legs that had just been waiting for her to remember, and she knew it wouldn't be long before her panties were clinging damply to her labia.

She unzipped her skirt and slipped out of it with practiced ease so she was standing in front of the class wearing only her knee-high black leather boots and black cotton bikini panties. The professor was holding her sweater, and now he took her skirt as well and casually draped them over the back of his chair before he began addressing his class, the slightly rough material of his own brown sweater very lightly grazing her as he gestured. She effortlessly tuned him out by remembering the way Patrick had pushed her back against the door and how tall and strong and inescapable he was; by remembering the thrill of his black leather coat coldly kissing her nipples. She loved the determined way he had taken control of her; it intensely excited her how helpless to resist him she was. If she had told him to stop he would have, she knew that; she had seen it in his eyes for over three years that he would never force himself on her, therefore his commanding attitude had turned her on instead of frightening her. In fact, she had been profoundly grateful for his firmness, it had aroused her as much (perhaps even more) as the way he kissed her and caressed her, rubbing her clit with the hard heel of his hand until she felt the beginnings of a climax forking a hot lightening between her juicing pussy and erect nipples... The rhythmic sound of the professor's voice instructing the class, numbering each point he was making, blended with what had happened to her last night and helped her understand how much she had learned about herself without even realizing it at the time.

"One..."

She obviously liked forceful men.

"Two..."

Big was definitely better. She would never forget her first and only glimpse of his cock when he pulled it out of his pants before she turned around and willingly positioned herself on the bed for him.

"Three..."

Having a sizable erection thrust fast and hard into her pussy was a stunningly pleasurable experience she most definitely wanted to suffer again.

"Four..."

She liked being given commands by a strong, handsome, confident man.

"Five..."

There was something to be said for older men. None of the young men she had slept with before (and there had been a few) ever fucked her like that...

She started slightly when a firm, cool pressure forced her out of her reverie as the professor began drawing on her chest just above and between her breasts. He was outlining the location and shape of her heart, the most important organ in her body. She sensed the blurry crowd of future surgeons watching attentively, and she smiled a little wondering how many of them were actually more interested in her erect nipples. It was slightly chilly in the room; she had an excuse for the taut, beautifully shaped breasts put on full display as they got delightfully in the professor's way when he began tracing the squat, cucumber-like shape of her spleen across the lower curve of her left mound and down over one of her ribs. His firm, assured caress was soothing... she flowed back into herself, and images of Patrick's powerful body kneeling fully clothed on the bed fucking her violently from behind gradually blended with the perverse intimacy she was enjoying with another older man as he exercised his knowledge and skills on her naked body. She was acutely aware of the slow rise and fall of her chest when his breathing warmed her breasts as he stood slightly bent over drawing her kidneys. Modeling for artists *was* very different; they never touched her, they caressed every inch of her intently, but only with their eyes. Today, however, her naked body was the canvas, and she liked it. The firm pressure of the pen's head pressing down on her skin in slow, circular caresses soothed her like a massage even as it stimulated her mind, full as it was with memories of being fucked like never before in her life.

She couldn't help it, the clean smell of the professor's soft brown hair, the ghostly trace of a pleasingly sweet tobacco buried in the pores of his skin, the hard line of his jaw as he concentrated, and especially the way his other hand rested firmly on the small of her back, it was all exciting her... a meltingly hot fantasy took root in her pelvis stimulated by the pressure of the pen tracing the outline of her bladder, his fingers so tantalizingly close to the most sensitive part of her. When he straightened up and grasped her arm to turn her slightly to one side, it was breathtakingly easy to imagine him bending her forward over the side of his desk and instructing her to hold still as he showed his students how to properly fuck a woman. Their notebooks forgotten, they all watched as their professor's exemplarily large cock slid into her tight little slot. She clung submissively to the edge of the desk, hanging her head, the muscles in her arms visibly straining and her dangling breasts quivering as he penetrated her. His initial slow, demonstrative rhythm swiftly escalated until he was pounding his penis into her ink-bloodied body, laying her open in front of a room full of young men with hard-ons straining jealously against their pants. She moaned quietly, hiding her face behind her hair as the force of the professor's thrusts undid the prim knot at the nape of her neck and a cool reddish-brown wave flowed over her shoulders. She closed her eyes, shyly unable to face what was happening even as her juicing pussy proved how much she secretly longed to be gang-banged...

The impersonal touch of the professor's hands should have been reassuring, but instead it profoundly distressed her in a way only totally hot daydreams could assuage. The deeper she fell into an unbridled erotic trance, the easier it was to do her best to please him as he continued caressing her with the cool, hard tip of his special red pen. Whenever his face entered her line of sight, she closed her eyes. She wasn't interested in his individual features and his tepid expression; the man he was in her fantasies was much more interesting. More arousing as well were the ideally handsome students populating the sexual classroom in her brain. Even the few females present figured into her imaginative fulfillment by being jealous of the fact that all the men wanted her and not them. And, she thought smugly, I'm getting paid for this.

"Turn around, please, Miranda."

"Yes, sir." It was so easy to imagine that he pushed her back across his desk, gripped her beneath the knees, and raised her open legs around him so he could sink his cock deep inside her again. She was forced to clutch the edges of the slick mahogany to brace herself against the force of his thrusts as three or four of the young men watching rose from behind their desks, erections visibly straining against their pants. They surrounded her where she lay helplessly pinned down by a penis plunging deeper and deeper into her hole even as it swelled and thickened until she thought she would die from the excruciating fulfillment of opening herself up to its stabbing rhythm. Then hands that were all as big and demanding as Patrick's began caressing her, hungrily squeezing her breasts and rubbing her clit right above the infinitely sensitive spot where the professor's cock was driving into her with growing urgency. Both her achingly hard nipples were engulfed in warm, lusty mouths as another tongue thrust between her lips, taking her breath away in a harsh, ravenous kiss that tasted just like Patrick's...

"Raise your arms over your head, please, Miranda."

She obeyed gracefully and in her fantasy two men roughly pulled her arms up over her head and pinned her down by the wrists as the professor rammed himself to a climax inside her, his erection buried deep in her belly. He had scarcely pulled out of her before another demanding cock slid easily into her hot wet cunt. She would have cried out if another man hadn't tilted her head back over the edge of the desk and slipped his dick between her lips. An almost unbearable pleasure germinated in her nipples as they were both relentlessly suckled while one man fucked her mouth and another her pussy, until she could no longer resist the orgasm that followed a devastating path along the red line the professor had drawn from her clit to her heart as all the organs he outlined seemed to dissolve...

"Thank you, Miranda, that will be all. You may get dressed now."

"Okay," she said, dreamily retrieving her clothing, not surprised he didn't lower himself to help her. But that was all right, she was being paid very well for letting him use her like this, and the truth was she had just used him in a much more enjoyable way. She wondered if any of the young men watching her walk over to the corner of her imaginary punishment could tell that her panties were wet and that her pussy – one of the few parts of her body that had not been discussed – was smoldering helplessly. She deliberately put her sweater back on first, leaving her skirt for last, because in those moments she seriously didn't know how she would react if her wild fantasy showed any signs of becoming hard fact.

Chapter Four

Michael unzipped his backpack and began pulling out his supplies. His hands were large, his fingers long and strong, and when they were stained with charcoal, they reminded him of his ancestors and the harsh, brutally basic lives they never had the power to rise above. He was supposed to have working man's hands meant to put food on the table for a big family, but their chosen struggle was to capture the human body on paper instead of just keeping it alive.

As one of the handful of males in the class, and the only attractive one, he was aware of the stir he caused whenever he walked in, and it both pleased and annoyed him. It made him feel strangely like a stereotype, uncomfortably two-dimensional. It also disappointingly made him question the talent of his fellow students, for such superficial perspectives did not a great soul and therefore a true artist make. They didn't know anything about him except that he looked like he belonged somewhere else. They were very wrong.

The schedule indicated they were working in colored charcoal today, and even though he preferred black, he enjoyed the solid rainbow the dusty colors made of his fingertips, and the inevitable streaks of war paint they left on his cheeks whenever he unconsciously scratched his three day-old dark-golden stubble as he concentrated, forgetting everything in the exciting battle of rendering the mysterious symmetry of beauty on paper.

He set his large sketchpad down on the wooden easel, flipping to the first blank page, and caressed the acid-free paper wistfully, wishing he might one day feel this way about a woman's flesh.

He was always acutely aware of his surroundings, of everything except looking like a master work himself. Unbeknownst to him, several of his female classmates had surreptitiously sketched him instead of the model. The jeans he invariably wore were a smooth charcoal black defining his tight ass and strong thighs. His long legs, narrow hips and broad shoulders had appeared with varying degrees of success on several canvases and sketchpads throughout the class. The instructor was a woman in her comfortable sixties and she believed her students should draw whatever inspired them. She also believed Michael had real talent, so apart from giving him some technical advice now and then she usually left him to his own devices.

He always felt a little like a kid as he laid his supplies out on the table beside the easel. The ritual invariably filled him with wonder and disbelief that responsible adults could actually spend so much time doing something fun. He also felt a stab of guilt wielded by his rigid upbringing and for an instant doubted his decision. For three generations the men of his family had all become police officers. The neat reverence with which he arranged his art supplies was inherited from his father; from watching him lay out his duty belt every night with its dark, heavy, inscrutable objects reflected in innocent five-year-old eyes. Later in life he was able to define the club, the gun, the handcuffs, all the common accoutrements of a cop, which he was not and would never be if he had his way. His was a different kind of discipline enforced upon the inner world of his desires, as dangerous and volatile as any real officer's beat. Certainly his family wanted him to believe he was doing the wrong thing by choosing art over law, but from a very early age Michael sensed he was related to the people around him by blood while some other equally vital connection was missing. In a way, he had been preparing himself for the decision to deviate from family tradition for as long as he could remember.

Social laws were not the ones that passionately interested him. He respected them, of course, but he wasn't fascinated by laws he could easily, blindly obey. The world of art – full of much more subtle yet mysteriously real laws governing a person's reaction to it – would take him a lifetime to master, perhaps more. That was a real challenge, especially when combined with the need to pay rent and put food on the table, as his mother would phrase it. It certainly beat spending his time cruising the streets contributing to global warming with the sole aim of putting deviants behind black iron bars. He much preferred the multicolored bars of his oil and charcoal pastels in which the only crime was to let them lie unused, their creative dimension unexplored.

He needed a haircut. The fact registered not because his mom told him so whenever he visited, but because he had to keep pushing it away from his face as he sketched. Sometimes after class, streaks of black and red (two of his favorite color combinations) in his blonde hair gave him the retro look of a punk rocker, except he didn't have enough piercings, just a small silver hoop in his left ear that had been there since he was seventeen and first openly rebelled against the future mapped out for him. Cops didn't wear earrings, the only silver hoops they were normally allowed were the hand-cuffs dangling from their belts. Women were attracted to cops, he knew that, he had suffered many long nights listening to his mother crying her-self to sleep when her husband didn't come home, and when he finally did, he always had an excuse even his innocent young son could sense was a clever fib. Infidelity was as much a part of a policeman's territory as the proverbial coffee and doughnuts.

Michael had just turned the legal age, but he had been aware of his cock, and all the things he could do with it, first by himself and then with girls, from a very early age. The fact that his dad was a cop had enhanced his nat-ural confident authoritative air, even when he was still fighting acne and jacking off alone every night. By the age of sixteen, he thought he had solved the mystery of what made a man attractive to women, until he met another girl and added her figure and feelings to the equation. He knew now just how hard a woman was to define in every sense.

Sketching the female body was a challenge he would never tire of. He spent hours at the MFA every week, not just to study and copy his favorite Masters, but because it also helped him save money on heat. He was friend-ly with most of the museum guards, some of which he had sketched, and whatever the reason, the pleasure with which they accepted their portraits was certainly not feigned. He didn't like to think that if it wasn't for the money his great-grandfather had left solely to him, he would be sitting in police academy now instead of watching a beautiful young woman step onto a small platform placed at the center of the room.

Her long, reddish-brown hair had been artfully pinned up by the instruc-tor in a Grecian style, a few naturally wavy ringlets escaping the gently con-tained, lustrously soft folds of her tresses. Her body was invisible beneath a white flannel blanket she held closed over her heart with both hands like a Vestal Virgin walking up the steps of the temple... Michael's imagination ran wild with her. History and Literature were his favorite subjects in high school, and suddenly a line from his freshman year production of *Romeo and Juliet*, in which he played the lead, came back to him, *For she doth teach the torches to burn bright*... There were only electrical lights shining steadily down upon her, but the over-the-top feelings of the character he had played years ago suddenly seemed believable. She stood poised in the center of the room surrounded by blank canvases all preparing to capture her, but none of them would, none of them possibly could. The instructor was right not to condemn this particular model to black-and-white, for her radiance could only be expressed with colors.

Michael glanced down at his charcoals in despair. He had not even begun, and already he knew he could never do her justice. Her skin alone was a marvel, glowing with youth, not creamy, not rosy, not olive-toned; no trite description could convey the supple luminosity of her flesh and the dramatic, tenacious way it clung to her delicate bones, all of them revealed as she opened the blanket and let it fall to her feet. A silent avalanche could not have been more devastating than that graceful gesture was to Michael. His classmates began dutifully sketching their subject of the day, plunging blithely into the impossible task of copying God's work. But it was a way of praising her, so he picked up his pencil and caressed her, beginning with the smooth angle of her brow dipping down into her eye sockets and rising out again into her cheek which flowed smoothly down into her chin as ideally as a cartoon princess' face. High cheekbones and large, slightly almond-shaped dark eyes the color of which he could not quite make out except he believed, he *felt*, they were green... the deepest green he had ever seen, beyond analogies, yet they inspired him to try... He had seen the ocean that color sometimes at the heart of summer during high tide, a deep, shimmering, self-contained green alive with undertows he was already getting carried away on...

Yes, those were the currents of thoughts he saw in her intense eyes, not normal, irrelevant preoccupations like fish darting just beneath the surface; her irises were ever so slightly unfocused, as if she was looking inside herself, deep inside at something profoundly interesting. She seemed completely unaware of the faces turned up towards her in varying degrees of concentration.

He always began with a model's face, moving from the head down. He couldn't understand people who began by sketching the shoulders or the legs or any other bodily parts before adding the head afterwards almost as an afterthought. He believed there weren't merely psychological reasons for his preference; it was visceral, almost metaphysical. He would worry about trying to flesh her out with colors later, at the moment he was too engrossed in her bone structure. Some might say her face was a little too narrow and her lips too full and her brow too pronounced, but they were wrong; her proportions felt perfect to him. He stroked her with his eyes as his pencil moved with increasing confidence across the paper. His hand worked steadily, his vision pressed against her flesh invisibly but possessively caressing her.

He shoved his hair away from his face and gripped the top of the sketch pad with his free hand. She was standing turned slightly away from him, and when the timer went off she would face in a different direction, but it wouldn't matter, he would have the best of her from any angle. He couldn't wait, he had to leave her beautiful face to outline the elegant length of her neck, and then the lovely dip of her shoulders where the bone perked up again gently before flowing down into her slender arms. When he began trying to capture her breasts he became fully conscious of his erection, and glad of the oversized black sweatshirt he was wearing. But that wasn't his biggest problem. Students weren't allowed to socialize with the models. Well, he didn't care. He came from a long line of cops, and part of him was already rising above the law.

Chapter Five

Patrick came again last night. He didn't bring his truck, and Miranda had no warning he was in the building until she heard his unmistakable knock. Minutes later, he was on her bed again still fully dressed, but this time lying on his back as she sat on his lap riding his cock.

Her breasts would have been bouncing up and down if he hadn't been hungrily kneading them like dough making him rise and harden even more deliciously inside her. She braced herself on his forearms, clinging to the rough material of his sweater wondering what his muscular chest would look like naked without actually wanting to see it. Dressed all in black with only his erection thrusting up out of his clothes, he turned her on more than any man ever had. The fact that only the most intimate parts of their bodies were caressing each other was for some reason exciting.

She was completely naked. He had stripped off her clothes the minute he walked through the door after a cursory glance around her apartment to make sure she was alone. He had spoken not a word, and she felt no earthly need to say anything as her blood purred contentedly beneath his rough handling. The synapses in her brain became confused, helplessly turned on by the violence of his desire for her. It made her feel perfectly, passively beautiful, with no burden of responsibility except to be mysteriously herself, which meant not resisting but instead being thrilled as he stripped her naked, swept her up in his arms, and carried her into the bedroom.

Her bedside lamp was on. She could see his eyes, and the intensity of his stare somehow imbued his penis with even more penetrating power. The rest of his body was motionless with concentration as his hips bucked up beneath her, driving his erection so far and so hard into her body her breathless cries wordlessly pleaded with him not to hurt her while her hot pussy juicing around his thrusts begged him not to stop. She was on top, but she wasn't riding his cock as he lay passively beneath her; he was still doing all the work, and she loved how strong he was. Then the sight of her breasts bobbing up and down when he let go of them to grip her hips made her start coming.

"Oh, yes, yes!" she gasped, reaching down to rub her clit hopefully, desperately. She felt her innermost flesh expanding around the demanding dimensions of his erection as never before... opening her up to a thoughtless state of profound enlightenment through the climax uncoiling slowly, inevitably, blessedly, in her pelvis. The intensifying fulfillment cut up her body as a beautiful heat sharper than a flaming knife following the devastating fault line of an orgasm. The pleasure was as awfully beautiful as the face of God, impossible to conceive of; it could only be endured as for transcendent moments her clitoris became much more than it seemed... it was a sun going nova and blinding her as she glimpsed a divine energy wrapped in the haunting gift of her flesh.

This is what her orgasm felt like now thinking about it as she stood before a class of aspiring artists. At the time, the pleasure had been too sear-ing in its intensity for thoughts as she came with Patrick sliding her pussy relentlessly up and down his hard-on. The only thing she could do to con-trol the joy was to take her working fingers off her clit, and lean forward against his chest in an effort to curve the excruciating power of the ecstasy claiming her spine like a lightning rod.

She was infinitely curious about her reactions to the way an older mar-ried man had fucked her. She had believed herself relatively experienced, that her disappointments and frustrations were natural and never destined to be assuaged until she met her soul mate. Yet Patrick was already another woman's destiny, not hers. She wasn't in love with him. That wasn't it...

While students sketched the different parts of her body, Miranda stood with one hand resting between her breasts and the other curved gently over her pussy as she pierced together the clues of a common working man's erotic power over her.

It had something to do with the fact that he never took his clothes off when he fucked her. He remained a stranger in black, a mysteriously pow-erful silhouette become flesh-and-blood just to possess her; forcing her to acknowledge her darkest desires before merging anonymously with the night again, leaving her alone in her lamp lit bedroom to face the conse-quences whatever they might be. Only the skin of his hands and of his cock, and of his mouth and of his tongue, ever came into contact with her, and it was hard to understand why this turned her on so much. Her naked body felt even more open to his forceful penetrations when she couldn't feel his bare flesh and reassure herself of his tenderness, of the fact that he would be kind and have mercy on her if how hard he was fucking her became too much for her. She was able to feel and perceive him as more than a man; as more than an erection caused by blood flowing into his groin and stiffening his otherwise soft and vulnerable organ. His hard-on was a force she could not resist, a force that penetrated her more deeply than any dick could ever reach physically, until she was crying out as if in agony, but actually because he was forcing her to come fully alive inside. And all this was possible because he was wearing black. A Hawaiian shirt and Bermuda shorts, for example, would have completely ruined the effect and his efforts.

The absence of endearments of any kind was also perversely stimulating. The fact that he told her more than once, almost angrily, how beautiful she was didn't count. His erection was as eloquent a statement as ever there was, and she was grateful he didn't ruin the devastating effect it had on her with sweet talk. She didn't want to be reassured that he loved her and wasn't going to hurt her, on the contrary.

Years of expensive psychotherapy could not have taught Miranda as much about herself, and the complex web of her emotional and physiological reactions, as her two brief encounters with Patrick had. She was fascinated by the discovery of these haunting erotic buttons in her psyche. In retrospect, she was beginning to realize they had always been there, but she had never before made love with a man who pushed them, whether he knew what he was doing or not. She suspected Patrick didn't fully understand why she behaved so submissively with him. The truth was, he didn't undress because he was in a hurry, because part of him felt guilty about what he was doing and therefore unconsciously limited their physical contact, reserving the tender intimacy of naked bodies resting in each other's arms for his wife. She didn't care. In her dimly lit bedroom, he was a dark and handsome stranger forcing her to accept his big hard cock...

The timer rang, jangling in her nerve ends as the reality of the art class in which she stood motionless as a statue came crashing back into her awareness.

She blinked a few times to get the distracting heads of students out of her eyes as she turned a few degrees to the right. A tall male figure snagged her attention, and once she looked his way she couldn't help but focus on his face. For a giddy moment she thought she was seeing Patrick the way he might have looked twenty or thirty years ago. The illusion lasted only half a second, for there was no doubt she had never felt the penetrating regard of those eyes before.

She did not break her pose; she held herself as regally motionless as before, but inside her emotions were in turmoil. She felt she knew him from somewhere yet at the same time it was obvious they had never met before because she would never have been able to forget him. Patrick had driven all thoughts of meeting her soul mate temporarily out of her mind, and this guy was much too superficially good-looking to be a profound part of her destiny, nevertheless, she couldn't take her eyes off him. She wasn't supposed to stare at the students drawing her, but at the moment the pencil in his hand wasn't moving over his sketch pad as he looked up at her face holding her eyes. It wasn't merely the external lines of her body he was studying; he was staring directly, boldly, into her eyes as if seeing inside her, letting her know he could and that he wanted to.

She lifted her chin slightly, defying him not to perceive that she was beautiful all the way through. She wasn't sure what that meant exactly, but she knew it was true. Then in the corner of her eye she saw the instructor moving towards him and quickly shifted her gaze as the old lady addressed him. Her heart was racing and her chest was tight with a fear bordering on anger that he was being reprimanded for staring at the model in an inappropriate way. She *wanted* him to keep looking at her that way!

Miranda never had a problem until then with the unspoken rule that she not date any of the students in order to avoid awkward complications, for example her boyfriend becoming jealous of the fact that so many other people saw her naked every day.

After a few minutes, she dared to turn her eyes back his way. The teacher had moved on and he appeared to be busy sketching again, but the way he smiled at her could in no way be described as impersonal. His firm mouth curled slightly up at the edges, forming two dimples in his cheeks she felt herself mysteriously falling into as if they were craters on the moon exerting an irresistible pull on her blood. His features were so regular they might have been boring if whatever created them hadn't sharpened and lengthened and filled them out in subtle ways that all added up to perfection on the virtual canvas of her visual cortex. The fact that he needed to shave only enhanced the strong line of his jaw, his five o'clock shadow a few shades deeper than his dark-blonde hair which was in need of a trim, she could tell because he kept running the fingers of his free hand through it, unconsciously showing off its soft fullness, its natural wave defying a straight cut without being chaotically curly. He was young, yet there was a gravity to his stance – to the determined way his boots were planted on the floor of the studio – that made him appear older than he probably was.

She hoped the teacher wasn't aware of their silent communication even as she couldn't bring herself to care. It was impossible for her to look away from him. It didn't even occur to her to be embarrassed by her nakedness. He obviously liked what he saw, and his expression made her wish there was more she could take off for him. A part of her brain warned her he was too handsome to be deep, that he was probably vain and arrogant and that an art class was just an easy credit for him. She tuned out these trite fears because they couldn't be true; if they were, she would be able to see through him. Her instincts almost always proved right in the end, especially when it came to men, and this guy was an exciting enigma, she could literally feel it in her womb as if their life together was being conceived right then and there.

Helplessly hooked on the secret smile he was openly sharing with her, she found herself thinking about the Little Mermaid who fell in love with a mortal male to her eternal detriment. Her best friend, Sarah, would take one look at him and declare, "This guy's trouble, Miranda, watch out!" but then again she hadn't told Sarah yet that she was fucking a married man nearly twice her age.

The class began to feel endless. She longed for it to be over so he could approach her, as she knew he would, as he absolutely had to do or she would die. She grew desperate for the hands of the clock to finally reach the right spot, especially after she became aware that heads were turning, following the direction of her eyes, which were normally misted by daydreams. *Of course*, she wasn't the only girl in the room who wanted him, yet there was also no doubt that standing before him naked gave her an advantage over them. He could see exactly what he was getting, even while the suspense remained intact because they had not yet even spoken to each other, must less touched.

He was dressed in black – a loose black sweatshirt, tight black jeans and black boots. She should have been able to picture him lying across her bed as she sat on his lap riding his cock, yet for some reason she could not. He wasn't Patrick; he wouldn't possess her in the same way. She had no idea how he would fuck her, it was like trying to see beyond the mountain she hadn't even begun to climb because first they had to meet, they had to speak to each other, and she had to know for sure he was interested in her or if, God forbid, this was all he cared to see of her. She closed her eyes, for a moment blinded by the dread he already had a girlfriend. A stunning guy like that couldn't possibly be unattached. She opened her eyes again. A girlfriend wasn't as big an obstacle as a wife.

Chapter Six

Miranda forced herself to do everything calmly, the way she normally would. It was a way of protecting herself from the intense joy of what was to come, or from a cataclysmic disappointment, both of which would disrupt the comfortable equanimity of her life. In a sense Patrick had already done that, but not to this degree; to the point where she felt in her bones that it was all or nothing. On the cosmic wheel of Fate, she fully expected to lose Patrick, and the thrill of playing a daring erotic hand was all she was after. It was different with this other man, she already knew that even though that was all she knew about him.

Upon arriving home, she carefully set the precious fragment of firm, acid-free paper he had given her beneath a dark-blue alabaster pyramid she used as a paperweight. She had guarded it all the way home on the bus and the train more passionately than a winning lottery ticket. Over and over again, she slipped her hand into the pocket of her coat, the one directly over her heart normally reserved for her ipod. She was in possession of his phone number. She felt like the luckiest girl in Boston.

It was incredibly difficult to resist the desire to call him the minute she walked through the door, but she was afraid he might not be home yet, and dreading the purgatory of an answering machine, she made herself wait. After turning on the heat, she peeled off her winter layers scarcely feeling the cold recalling the strong warmth of his grip. She didn't need a shower this evening; she suffered a hot flash of excitement deep between her legs every time she remembered how he had been waiting for her out in the hallway…

After she finished dressing behind a folding screen, she walked out of the studio feeling completely numb because she thought he had left. She had watched him through one of the narrow slits impatiently leaping from one foot to the other as she tugged her tights back on as fast as possible. She saw him efficiently put all his supplies away and easily hoist the heavy pack onto his back. How quickly he moved filled her with despair that he wasn't giving her time to catch up with him. She was still half naked as he strode towards the classroom door, not even glancing at the Oriental work of art behind which she stood struggling with all the layers of clothing her body needed to survive, but nothing could protect her from the cold terror that he was leaving her behind before they had even met. After she saw him walk out the door, she finished dressing with the calm of absolute despair. He was gone. He had seen all he wanted to see of her. His beautiful girlfriend was probably waiting for him outside in an expensive car her daddy bought her wearing a tight sweater showing off her big breasts. Of course he wasn't interested in slumming it with a poor artist's model who had to take a bus and a train to work and who didn't even need a bra her breasts were so small. She slipped into her coat, and wound the scarf around her neck furiously three times. On the first loop she was a fool for letting her imagination run away from her, as usual. On the second loop he was a bastard for leading her on with that secret, seductive smile promising her so much to come. On the final loop, a miserable disappointment hit her in the chest with such force she could hardly breathe for a moment. Tears welled up in her eyes she brushed furiously aside with the back of her ungloved hand. "Good night, Miranda, lovely job dear, as always," the instructor said as she hurried past her desk. "Good night!" she mumbled, and shoved open the door leading out into the hallway wrapped in a protective numbness she needed to get her home before she acted like a complete idiot and broke down over a total stranger. The sight of him leaning against the wall waiting for her made her gasp and stop dead as if she had just received a blow to her soul; the intensity of the relief that overwhelmed her was almost painful. She didn't have time to be embarrassed by the naked joy of her reaction before he pushed himself away from the wall and grasped her hand, squeezing it hard, his face enticingly close to hers as he looked down into her eyes. He wasn't smiling as he pressed a scrap of paper against her palm, and then walked away down the hall without bothering to look back. She didn't even think of following him. She stood happily rooted to the spot gazing down at the numbers of her own personal cosmic jackpot.

Miranda poured herself a glass of Chardonnay, but there was no denying that her red cordless phone had become the heart of her apartment. His promisingly unique pulse was waiting for her on the other end. She was nervous, not just because she felt this was such an important phone call, but because she was afraid Patrick might show up again. It was getting close to the time when she had heard his knock on the door last night.

Walking over to the living room window, she parted the heavy red velvet curtain and gazed anxiously down at the dark street. Surely he wouldn't leave his wife home alone three nights in a row? She fervently hoped not, because if he knocked when she was talking on the phone she would have to pretend not to be home. Who did he think he was anyway, showing up whenever he felt like it to fuck her. Then he just took off with a tight, hard look on his face that threatened to make *her* start feeling guilty, for Christ's sake, when he was the one being unfaithful to someone while she was simply being true to herself by daring to have new and exciting experiences. His was the crime of adultery, not hers. Although in the eyes of society she was an accomplice to the fact, in her opinion everything was too subtle and complex to be so easily judged. His wife could also be guilty for not satisfying him sexually, and so forth and so on in an endless web of circumstances and experiences, thoughts and feelings, dreams and fantasies, hopes and fears.

The street was quiet. It was time to pick up the phone and dial Michael's number. She did so slowly and carefully as if entering the combination of a safe containing everything she could ever hope for in a man. He had spelled his name out for her in an elegant cursive, the *M* rising high as triumphal arches over the city rooftops of the vowels and consonants housing his identity. *Michael…* Such a common name for someone who already felt so mysteriously special.

She took another quick sip of wine as the phone rang on the other end, and rang again, then again. She braced herself to hang up before an answering machine picked up…

"Michael speaking."

"Michael?" she said stupidly.

"Yes?"

"Hi, it's Miranda… you gave me your number…"

"Ah, yes, Miranda… I'm glad you called."

An incredulous laugh escaped her. "Did you ever doubt I would?"

"Where there's hope there's doubt, although there's no doubt about the fact that you're incredibly beautiful, Miranda."

"Oh, please… thanks…"

"You do realize how beautiful you are, don't you?"

She smiled. "Yes, I suppose I do."

"Good."

"Why?"

"Because false modesty is a waste of time and energy, and there's a lot better things we could be doing with our energy."

Her broad smile was beginning to hurt the muscles of here face, unaccustomed to stretching so far; she couldn't remember ever feeling this happy before. "I agree, Michael."

"That's nice." He lowered his voice suggestively, "Why don't you give me an example."

She giggled. "I don't know you well enough…"

"Do you really feel that way?"

"No, actually, I don't…"

"How *do* you feel?" he asked even more quietly.

"I don't know… I feel like I know you… somehow…"

"Maybe you do, Miranda, and the mind and body you're inhabiting at the moment just doesn't remember."

She couldn't keep the delight out of her voice, "You believe in reincarnation?"

"It's as good a theory as any. I believe a part of us survives."

"You mean like the energy composing our bodies," she kept her tone carefully neutral, "you know, the electrons and protons and neutrons, and whatever, merging with all the other sub-atomic particles shaping reality as we know it after our body decays, so that maybe a little but of us survives in a tree, another in a rock, our big toe in a bush, etc?"

"No, I'm talking about the soul, Miranda."

"Thank God, because, really," she confessed fervently, "I wouldn't find that other unconsciously dispersed form of survival very satisfying at all."

"So you were testing me?"

Her smile died. "No... I mean..."

"Never mind, but in the future, Miranda, I would appreciate it if you would simply ask me what you want to know instead of trying to trap me into saying what you want to hear."

"I'm sorry... I promise, Michael." *In the future...* Coming form him they were the most wonderful words in the world.

"But why are we talking about death?"

"I don't know. I thought we were talking about eternal life."

"You're right, we were, and I'm not surprised, even though I've never had a first conversation like this with a girl before in my life."

"Is that good?"

"What do you think?"

"I think you sound pleased, Michael."

"I am."

"I'm glad."

"Would you like to please me, is that what you're saying, Miranda?"

His voice was flowing straight down into her pussy where its deep, insinuating warmth was causing lightning-like flashes of desire that made it increasingly difficult for her to think clearly. "Yes, Michael..."

"Yes, *what*, Miranda?"

"I want to please you, Michael."

"I'd like to take you out to dinner. Can you meet me in Harvard Square in two hours?"

"Yes." She would meet him anywhere.

"You know where *Grendel's* is?"

"Yes…"

"I'll wait for you at the bar, then we'll get a table."

"Okay. Do you have a cell phone number, just in case-"

"No, but don't worry, sweetheart, I'll be there."

Chapter Seven

Sarah Dressor sat at her favorite table in a corner of *Grendel's*. She spent hours there reading, writing, and nibbling on Pita bread modestly dipped in the plate of Hummus that could last are all night if she wanted. She had become a fixture of the place, like a character in a sitcom, except that *she* was the silent audience and everybody else was a character on a stage it amused her to observe and cast wry judgment upon. In her opinion, few people merited an Oscar for the performance of their lives. She was superficially acquainted with a handful of regulars like herself, but mostly she knew nothing about the countless souls that tromped in and out of the quaint underground restaurant. A good percentage of the clientele naturally came from the University, students in noisy groups, or accompanied quietly by their parents visiting from out of town, and of course the occasional professor, either by himself or with his wife, neither of them looking too happy with life. Unfortunately, tourists often stumbled upon the Square's little secret. Anyone who appeared to be from the mid-west Sarah ignored completely as beyond her understanding. A hard-working Iowa farmer and a young intellectual Jewish woman living off a Trust Fund were worlds apart, and so she left them alone in her brain as she would aliens from outer space, although (in her firm opinion) she probably had more in common with travelers from another planet than with people from Fargo.

She was ostensibly working on her thesis as she sipped a glass of red wine that also lasted her for hours. She had been working on her thesis for three years. She was studying Comparative Religion at Harvard. Such a profound subject could not be rushed. Her mother, who had committed suicide when her daughter was just thirteen-years-old, would not understand her choice of subject matter, or most likely she would be indifferent to it. Then again (Sarah had pondered the thought most of her adult life) how could you kill yourself if you weren't at least subconsciously hoping you would end up in a better place? Nothingness, the complete absence of consciousness, struck her as a much worse deal than anything life could dole out. Although maybe not, because pain was definitely hard to bear; the kind of pain her diabetes, if she wasn't very careful, sometimes made her suffer in the form of ungainly sores; infections no one would ever know about except her and her doctors, and her best friend. She enjoyed winter mainly because she could wear gloves to hide her chipped and sickly yellow fingernails.

She was not making much progress on her thesis tonight because of the guy sitting at the bar. Now *that* was a man she could write an epic poem about. She lived in a college town, handsome young men were not uncommon, but her eyes and her instincts told her he was much more than that; she sensed right away he was not your typical student. She shifted slightly in her chair, leaning back against the brick wall to better study him unobserved in between the leaves of a hanging plant. His black jeans fit him like a dream, but they were faded; old. He either wasn't rich or he liked to play the Bohemian. His broad shoulders and tight black turtleneck sweater evoked the original Saint played by Roger Moore, but that was where the resemblance ended because his features were not so primly delicate; they were strong, the cliché "rugged" came to mind, and yet that was wrong, too. Viking kings might have had faces like that, except there was an elegant tenderness to his mouth beneath the classical perfection of his nose that made her think dreamily of ancient Greece and the sensual glory of the Renaissance. He was sitting alone, but he kept glancing at the door. He was waiting for someone, and not a friend. He was expecting a girl. Every line of his body was taught, poised to make a kill tonight even as he leaned against the bar looking sexily relaxed, both his hands cupped loosely in a man's favorite form of prayer around a glass of Guinness. He had good taste in beer at least, no bottled Michelob or Budweiser for him, thank you very much, he was drinking from the tap even if it was a bit more expensive and his money would be better spent on a new pair of jeans.

Sarah licked her dry lips and took another sip of wine, enjoying it as her mind began wandering wickedly. She imagined that if she walked past him she wouldn't be completely invisible to him, as she was to most men. He would see, and even appreciate, her diaphanous flowing veils reminiscent of Salome, and he would smile listening to the musical jingling of her myriad costume bracelets. His eyes would move up from her shapely legs to her full breasts and the nice cleavage exposed by her twenties-style Flapper dress. Not until he reached her face would disappointment flicker in his eyes and cause him to look away. She wasn't *ugly*, she had full rosy cheeks and big vulnerable brown eyes, but her already thinning hair was a frizzy lifeless brown she could do nothing about except hide it beneath a hat. Maybe the male animal, no matter how dumb, could sense she was not of healthy childbearing stock. She was realistically prepared to die before she turned fifty, and she could certainly never have children, all the more reason why it seemed so unfair she should be denied life's greatest pleasure – being fucked by a truly beautiful man. She had a string of ex-boyfriends, but they meant no more to her than the dirt-cheap Mardi Gras necklaces she always wore, string upon string of gold, red, purple, green and black beads as if she was a female peacock. Vibrant colors helped support her when she felt weak and tired and profoundly drab. Her abundant jewelry made her feel bright and alive the way she didn't at night when she took it all off and was left alone with her medicines and unending health problems.

If she could just get this guy alone, she might, if she focused all her charm and wit on him, be able to seduce him. Men had told her more than once what a talented mouth and gloriously yielding throat she had. All she need-ed was a few minutes alone with him to show him what a plain but highly intelligent and absolutely shameless girl could do. She would fall to her knees behind him, surprising him, and he wouldn't stop her as she tugged down his jeans and underpants. Then with both hands she would part the tight, muscular cheeks of his ass and gave him the rimming of his life. It would be an honor to have her less than beautiful features buried in his sub-lime butt-crack. She would thrust the pointed tip of her tongue hungrily into his gorgeous ass; shuddering, it would glide up inside him deeper and deeper, lustfully fucking him. Then, imperfect as she was, she would clone herself just so she could suck his cock at the same time that she licked his ass, trapping him in a vice of pleasure as he both penetrated and was pene-trated, his erection swelling in the soft, warm depths of her mouth even as she thrust her hot tongue into his darkly delicious anus...

He was about to come in her fantasy and flood her throat with the evi-dence of what a good little cock-sucker she was when he abruptly slipped off the bar stool, and walked quickly towards the person who had just entered the restaurant. It was a girl, of course… it was Miranda!

Instinctively, Sarah raised her arm to wave a greeting, but as she was about to happily cry out her friend's name, she stopped herself. They were obviously on a date; it would be rude of her to intrude.

She watched them just stand there for a moment staring into each other's eyes, and envy blossomed, hot and agonizing, in her chest because she knew in her brittle bones that no man would ever look at her like that, nor would she be able to look at someone that way herself. *Oh Miranda, Miranda!* She thought. *Watch out! This guy can break your heart without even trying.* But she was honest enough with herself to add, *Or he might just be the one you've been waiting for.* Her lovely friend's belief in true love had amused Sarah to no end when they first met, but the longer she knew Miranda, the more she couldn't help respecting her friend's faith in what she called the "Magic Pattern". Miranda was unlike anyone she had ever met. At first Sarah reasoned that when you were born that beautiful it was easy to have faith in the universe, especially when you also came from a happy, loving family, an adored single child of parents now tritely living in Florida. In the beginning, Sarah cherished the cynical opinion that Miranda had turned out as good as gold only because she was poor, but years of friendship had gradually broken down the walls of her jealous defenses until she accepted her place as the handmaiden of a true princess. She could never share Miranda's faith in the beneficent nature of the universe, but how passionately creative, and how absolutely honest and lacking in any hidden agenda Miranda was made Sarah more than willing to hope.

Oh, good, she thought with voyeuristic glee as the beautiful couple seated themselves at a table directly in her line of sight. They couldn't see her in the shadows; she could observe them to her heart's content for a while. There was a striking presence about them that was part of, and yet mysteriously more, than their stunning good looks.

Not surprisingly, they too ordered the Hummus appetizer. Miranda loved Hummus so much she made her own at home every week. As if her looks weren't enough, she was also an incredible cook. But worst or best (depending on Sarah's mood) Miranda wrote metaphysically penetrating, thought-provoking poetry. And from the way her date was looking at her, it was clear he was smart enough to know what a treasure he had sitting across from him. Her reddish-brown hair waving softly down her back seemed to light up the room, catching the candlelight in its flaming depths. As usual she was wearing solid colors, and tonight she had chosen a forest-green sweater that brought out her eyes, the fine cashmere clinging to her erect nipples in an innocently sexy way. Beneath it she wore her favorite knee-length black wool skirt and her beloved black leather boots, and as she curved a stray strand of hair behind a shell-like ear, Sarah glimpsed a luminous tear-shaped pearl, the only jewelry competing with her natural beauty.

They had ordered a bottle of red wine and were deep in conversation. Somehow they managed to eat and drink without taking their eyes off each other. Sarah couldn't stand it another second. She pushed herself up out of her chair and approached them.

"Miranda!" She feigned surprise.

"Sarah!"

"You didn't tell me you'd be here tonight," she accused mildly, smiling.

"She didn't have time," her date replied in a very deep, very quiet voice that made Sarah grab the back of a chair to steady herself against its mysterious impact.

"Well, I don't want to interrupt..."

"You're not interrupting." Only Miranda could lie with such a ring of truth in her voice. But then maybe it *was* true. What was a mere mortal to a god and goddess who had finally found each other despite all the stars and light years in their path? "Michael, this is my best-friend, Sarah."

"Pleasure to meet you, Sarah." He smiled up at her. "Won't you join us?"

"I've already ordered…" She glanced back at her dark table in the corner.

"Just for a minute," Miranda urged, cleverly being generous even while setting a time limit on the intrusion.

"Okay, maybe for a minute." Sarah seated herself next to her friend.

"Excuse me for a moment please, ladies." Michael stood up, and both girl's watched him walk away to the men's room.

"Okay, where the hell did you find him?" Sarah demanded.

"He found me, actually." Miranda was smiling beatifically. "He's an art student."

"He's seen you naked?!"

"Yes."

"God!" Sarah closed her eyes. "You stood in front of a guy like that *naked*? How did you not just *die?*"

"I've never felt more alive!"

"I'll bet!"

"We just met this afternoon… Sarah, I've been very bad lately."

"*Do* tell."

"Seriously… I've been fucking a married man."

"He's married?!"

"No! Not Michael!"

"Who?"

"The heating oil man."

"What did you say? I could *not* have heard you correctly, Miranda."

"Michael can't ever find out!"

"Oh, yes, you mean that tall, handsome older man? I was at your apartment one night when he filled your tank, I remember him now… Hmm, I'd fuck him, too."

"My mom always told me I would never meet my soul mate until I stopped thinking about him and waiting for him all the time, and she was right, Sarah. I was all wrapped up in thoughts of Patrick when I suddenly looked down at the class and saw him, Michael, I mean."

"You just met him and you're already sure he's your soul mate?"

"Yes, and don't get all cynical and protective of me, Sarah. I've *never* felt this way before. The minute I saw him it was as if I had always known him. I know he's the one, I know it. I can feel it."

"God forbid I should argue with the logic of your feelings."

'Now you're being sarcastic."

"Oh, *no*."

"He's coming…"

"I'll leave you alone with him."

"Do you mind, Sarah? We only just met…"

"Only if you promise to call me tomorrow and tell me everything, and I mean everything."

"You know I will."

"Good luck, sweetie. I love you."

"I love you, too."

Sarah quickly got up and left the table before Michael had the chance to politely try and persuade her to stay, because she would find it impossible to deny him anything.

Chapter Eight

A girl like this was a gift, a blessing, a miracle, and whether or not God was responsible was not a debate Michael cared about at the moment. If what was sitting before him was a random combination of electrons and protons and neutrons and vibrating strings, then he was seriously impressed with the creative powers of pure chance. He had heard the term "a complete package" used to describe women who were intelligent as well as beautiful, but calling Miranda "a complete package" was like casually cataloguing an ancient statue that once graced the heart of a temple unearthed in pristine condition in the 21st century. From the moment he saw her, his imagination had been running wild with images. She was none of these things with which he tried to describe the impact she had on him because she was simply everything. There was no escaping this astonishing and, he had to admit, frightening realization.

He was not remotely ready to settle down with one woman, the thought had not even crossed his mind except as a vague longing for the future, but here she was. Every inch of her was beautiful, until she laughed and talked, then she was so much more than the sum of her parts. The combination of her smile and her eyes staring so intently into his made it necessary for him to look away from her every few minutes. There was only one ultimate question, one longing, shining in her ocean-deep irises, and he could tell she believed he had the power to answer it. He wanted to shoulder such a potentially pleasurable responsibility, but part of him was holding back somewhat. His life was difficult enough as it was defying his parents and stretching his unlikely inheritance as far as he could to make it last. He might very well end up a cop in the end, but he was giving himself a decade to try and find a way out of that regimented fate. He could barely afford the loft space he was renting. It was just large enough to accommodate his bed, a kitchenette, all his easels and art supplies, a small television and a stereo. There was no room for a girl like Miranda.

"What are you thinking, Michael?" she asked suddenly, her radiant smile dimming un uncertain degree.

"Oh a million things at once, sorry."

"Why should you be sorry?"

"I'm not." He returned her smile. "You inspire a lot of thoughts, Miranda" He reached over and covered one of her hands with his where it rested on the table. He had only grasped her hand once before in the hallway outside the studio, but the sensation of her fingers weaving themselves between his felt alarmingly natural, as though they had held hands a thousand times before. "You're so beautiful," he added in an undertone, feeling a little foolish about repeating himself; he had told her this at least twice since they sat down. It was worth it, however, to watch her glance away shyly as a glow that could only be described as the visual equivalent of a purr made her face even lovelier. "Will you sit for me in private, Miranda?"

She looked deep into his eyes again as she replied, "I would love to, Michael."

A true artist was able to possess beauty from the inside out. A true artist had the power to make the soul of beauty take form beneath the caress of his pencil or brush. A true artist had to be *possessed* by beauty, to worship it in every sense of his being. Michael suspected he had talent because he was obsessed with the reality of beauty. The symmetry of two lines intersecting in space was mysteriously beautiful. A girl like Miranda was the pinnacle of infinite intersections of molecules and genes and chromosomes and every other subatomic pigmentation identified by science. Beauty could never be possessed, it could only be worshipped in the form of unending works of art, cherished and protected. Yet he could see it in her eyes that she wanted, that she longed, to be possessed.

"You've gotten very quiet, Michael. Is something wrong? I'm sorry if I'm blabbing, I know I can just talk and talk."

"You're not blabbing." He squeezed her hand. "I love listening to you."

She laughed. "I can't even remember what I was just talking about."

"It doesn't matter."

"It's just that... I feel you understand everything I'm saying, Michael. Most guys just-"

"I'm not most guys."

"I know," she agreed fervently.

He was suddenly uncomfortably aware of Sarah pretending not to stare at them from her introverted corner of the restaurant. "Do you need to get up early tomorrow, Miranda?"

"No, I don't..."

He relished the sight of her body subliminally tensing as her eyes grew softer and darker, vulnerable, profoundly yielding. The slight glimmer of fear and the depth of longing in her gaze made him even more aware of how uncomfortably his cock had been pressing against the crotch of his jeans all evening looking at her. He was torn between the desire to sketch the graceful curve of her flesh where her neck flowed into her shoulder, and a beastly urge to sink his teeth into her luscious slenderness. And the way the tear-shaped pearls in her ears trembled when she laughed and moved her head had him savoring the thought of the tender rosy pearl of her clit secreted away in the most intimate folds of her flesh. "Then how about if we head out of here," he suggested, "pick up a bottle of wine somewhere, and continue this conversation at your place?"

"No need to pick up a bottle, I've got plenty of wine at home."

Her response reassured him he wasn't moving too fast for her, and her trusting compliance made his hard-on respond in such a away that he was forced to think unappealing thoughts for a few seconds. He further distracted himself by calling the waitress over and paying the bill. It pleased him that his lovely date didn't offer to go Dutch with him. She obviously didn't have problems with traditional roles, and not because she was stupid, on the contrary. She was profoundly confident enough not to realize how free she was from the usual doubts and worrisome considerations that constantly plague ordinary human beings.

"Will you let me read some of your poetry, Miranda?" he asked as he signed the credit card receipt.

"Of course. I'll give you some to take home."

"You wouldn't read some for me?"

"I'd rather not..."

He loved it when she glanced away like that, it was endearingly sweet and gave him the chance to study the exquisite lines of her profile. He kept his voice low, "What if I *command* you to read me a poem?"

"Then I will, Michael," she answered just as quietly.

"Why are you so shy about your work?"

She shrugged.

"Well, I won't make you do anything you're uncomfortable with," he promised, but his cock was sending him other, very different thoughts. Her resistance was as refined and complex as a painted Japanese parasol, there was no need for him to crush it, he would simply, gradually fold her in on herself until she realized the single most important thing she wanted out of life was to do whatever he told her to.

* * *

He watched her walk across the living room and part a red curtain hanging over a window looking down on the street. She seemed anxious. He wondered if he should leave. Then she turned back towards him and laser-blasted all concerns out of his mind with that smile of hers. No one had ever made him feel so special. Most girls couldn't resist him, and she was no exception, but standing in the middle of her living room he felt taller, mysteriously noble, more centered in himself and his unique destiny than ever.

"You have a very nice place here, Miranda." He slipped off his black leather jacket.

"Thank you." She immediately took the heavy, supple leather from him and hung it up next to her coat. "I bought most of my furniture at thrift stores," she confessed with a hint of pride; not a trace of shame. Over dinner she had told him about her landlady and the incredible deal she was getting on rent. He was not surprised. He hadn't even known her twenty-four hours and he was already inspired to do whatever he could for her.

"Please have a seat while I pour us some wine," she urged.

"I'd rather come with you."

"Okay."

He followed her into the kitchen. Their bodies remained only inches apart, they *had* to; there was a magnetic attraction between them neither one of them was remotely inclined to resist.

"Should we stick with Merlot?" she asked, bending over to open a cupboard.

He watched her hair tumble forward in a smoldering wave that just begged to be painted. The lovely ass he had suffered a painful erection sketching earlier in the day was now thrust invitingly up into the air just inches away from his hand. He couldn't resist reaching over and caressing it as she gazed up at him questioningly. "Merlot will be fine," he spoke softly, holding her eyes as he stroked the smooth contours of her bottom through the slightly rough wool of her skirt.

She looked away, reaching into the cabinet for a bottle, and he took a cautious step back, giving her space to straighten up again. He had seen in her eyes what he already knew – she was going to let him fuck her tonight. He could take his time, he could savor the certainty of her submission and make her wait for his cock until her eyes were begging him to take her, to penetrate her, to do whatever he wanted to her...

He deliberately slipped his hands into the pockets of his jeans to let her know she was safe for the time being as she reached up to open another cabinet for some glasses. Now he was treated to the sight of one of her pert breasts outlined beneath the tight cashmere shirt she was a very clever and very cruel girl to have worn without a bra. The vision of her firm, well defined nipples had been driving him half crazy all evening. He would make her pay for it later.

She didn't ask him what he was thinking; what he was smiling about. He was willing to bet her pussy was wet. He could tell her juices were flowing for him by how careful she was with her movements as she uncorked the bottle, and filled both glasses with a liquid that so very much resembled the blood of their hearts beating faster and harder with the knowledge that very soon their bodies would become one.

"Thanks." He claimed one of the glasses from the counter and walked ahead of her back into the living room. He seated himself on the cream-colored loveseat half covered by a cashmere throw of dark, spiraling designs. She perched beside him, keeping her knees together as she sipped her wine almost primly, and her school girl-like shyness turned him on dangerously.

"I'm surprised you don't have a cat," he remarked, once again looking around him at the eclectically furnished, immaculately maintained space. Nothing matched in the traditional sense, yet the result was a pleasing whole achieved by a harmony of complimentary and contrasting colors and textures.

"No pets allowed," she explained, taking another nervous sip of wine.

He set his glass down on a small circular marble table. "Look at me, Miranda."

She also set her glass down, on the table beside her made of multicolored glass squares supported by four black wrought iron legs, and obeyed him.

"You look nervous," he observed gently, caressing the hair away from her face and letting his fingertips linger on the cool softness of her temple.

"I'm not," she said faintly, licking her lips invitingly.

"Do you want me to leave?" He rested his hand on one of her knees.

She let her legs fall open. There was no need for her to say anything. Her body's response was infinitely more eloquent as she fell back against the loveseat and allowed his hand to move slowly up her inner thigh towards her pussy. But the black tights she was wearing protected her, he couldn't feel her skin, and it suddenly made him almost angry.

"Take off your shirt," he said. It was cold in her apartment, but he didn't care, in fact, he was glad. He wanted her nipples to stay hard; to be as sensitive as possible to his touch and the warm, hungry licks of his tongue.

She obeyed him gracefully, sitting up and pulling her sweater off over her head in one smooth gesture. She was an expert at undressing. She was accustomed to men, and even other women, seeing her naked. And there was that exquisite torso again, so slender, so fine-boned, so ideally shaped, with breasts that made him think of a Titian Venus, so round and pointed, so delicate and full, all at the same time.

He pushed himself off the loveseat and sank to one knee before her as he gathered her wafer-white bosom hungrily in both hands. He deliberately let her nipples briefly taste his lips before he pressed her back against the cushion with the force of his kiss. He thrust his tongue into her mouth, squeezing her luscious little tits and brushing the balls of his thumbs over her straining nipples. He was falling... falling from a bottomless height and crash landing against her soft warmth... and the more fearlessly he plunged into her, the more yielding she became...

He forced himself to pull back, and raising his hands from her breasts cupped her face instead. "Do you want me to make love to you?" he whispered.

She nodded fervently, as if literally placing all her thoughts and feelings in his hands.

Chapter Nine

When Miranda awoke the next morning, the world outside had been transported during the night into the heart of a fairytale. When she parted her red curtains she saw snow falling from the dark sky slowly and silently, surrounding the tower of her building with a pure white wall no mortal man could breach. But it didn't matter because her prince was already sleeping warm and naked beneath her white sheets and the soft feathery drift of her comforter.

She stood at the window in her black robe and slippers wondering why an element as deadly and treacherous as snow embodied the very soul of coziness, especially around Christmas. It had to be the intense contrasts – inside warmth and light and color safely defying the absolute silence and emptiness outside. In a photographic negative snow is as black as the universe before life began.

In the bedroom, Michael was sleeping as deeply as he penetrated her last night, all his hard energy resting now in soft cotton flannel sheets deliciously warmed by their combined body heat.

She clutched the robe more tightly closed over her heart breathing a sigh of relief. He wouldn't leave. The buses would be running with hour long delays today if it kept snowing this way. And Patrick was all the way out in Dorchester. He couldn't just show up at her door in a storm like this no matter how hot he was for her. She was safe for the day, the snow was protecting her, and the feeling growing within her.

She hadn't fully realized how lonely she was until Michael filled the void inside her with his presence. Her pussy had clung passionately to his cock, her innermost muscles embracing it as they never had another. When Patrick fucked her she opened herself passively to his thrusts, but she was not inspired to milk him the way she did Michael's hard-on. There was a slight, deeply stimulating curve to his penis, and the distinct way his head was carved from his shaft made it exquisitely easy for her labial lips to suck on it in desperate delight before he slipped his full length inside her, or whenever he pulled almost all the way out of her to tease and torment her. Patrick's erection was perhaps a little bigger than the younger man's, but it was perfectly straight, the head merging with the rest like a ramming rod he used to great effect, but without any of the sensual character Michael put into his love-making.

Miranda left the curtains open to frame the storm and turned reluctantly away from the window. She loved watching it snow. Snow was freedom, freedom from school when she was a little girl and freedom from work now that she was a little older. Snow was a reprieve from time... the seconds and minutes of the day froze and fell away leaving only the hauntingly cozy depth of the present. Responsibilities were temporarily buried and all she had to do was marvel at the warmth of her body and her home, mysteriously one and the same thing to her soul, especially on this wondrous day when everything she could possibly want on this earth was inside with her.

She moved quietly as a cat in her kitchen so as not to disturb the man sleeping in her bedroom. He looked as beautiful to her as a young god miraculously fallen from heaven into her arms. The first time his cock slid inside her, she cried out from the shock of how perfectly he filled her up. There wasn't a hint of discomfort; the dimensions of his erection conformed ideally with the shape and depth of her pussy, opening gratefully to this long awaited fulfillment of her physical and deepest selves simultaneously. She had always dreamed it would be like this, that the penetrations of the man she was meant to be with would feel like no other's. The way his eyes looked so deeply into hers made all the difference to her body's response, her sex mysteriously lubricated by her soul's attraction to his and the intensely silent way they communicated as their naked bodies began rocking together, easily finding their rhythm, like a silent music heard by all the special nerve ends coming fully alive where their flesh merged into one.

Great sex and a snow storm were classic excuses for a big hot breakfast. She couldn't begin cooking until he woke up, but she could enjoy laying everything out in preparation. She filled the tea pot so it was ready to brew, set her small wooden table with the colorful cloth napkins and bamboo placemats she had been saving for a special occasion, and she even pulled out the silverware inherited from her maternal grandmother. The white porcelain cow that until now had served only as decoration became pregnant with a decadent amount of heavy cream, and she took a stick of butter out of the fridge so it would soften up and spread a sinfully smooth layer of animal fat on their whole wheat bread. Finally, she placed an omelet pan on the gas stove, and set a bag of mixed vegetables out on the counter to defrost.

Running out of things to do, Miranda at last returned to the dark bedroom. With Michael there it felt warm and cozy as an enchanted cave, the old-fashioned radiator every once and a while emitting a dragon-like hiss of steam. He was her black knight. She scooped his black jeans and black sweater off the floor and draped them reverently over a chair. She then spread her robe on top of them, kicked off her slippers, and slipped back into bed with him.

He rolled over onto his back, clutching the sheets to his chest, and she watched, smiling, as his eyes opened to gaze blankly up at the ceiling.

"Good morning," she said quietly, nudging him gently back into consciousness.

He turned his head on the pillow. "Good morning." His voice was hoarse as he dragged it up from the depths of sleep, but his eyes were wide awake now looking at her.

Her smile faded. He was staring at her so soberly the weight of the snow falling outside almost began to feel oppressive. "Did you sleep okay?" she asked inanely, hiding her anxiety about what he was thinking.

"Yes, I did." He sounded surprised.

"I'm glad."

He raised his arm. "Come here."

She snuggled happily up against him, resting her head on the hard yet wonderfully comfortable pillow of his chest and shoulder. "Is everything all right?" she found the courage to ask.

"Everything is much more than all right, don't you think?"

"Oh, yes." She sighed. "It's snowing really hard outside."

"Is it?"

"Mm-hmm. There's already at least six inches on the ground and it doesn't look like it's going to stop anytime soon."

"I guess that means I'm trapped here. What a terrible fate."

"Yes, I conjured up this storm just to keep you here with me. I'm a powerful sorceress, am I not?"

"The most beautiful and powerful sorceress of all. I'm in your thrall, Miranda Covington."

She didn't laugh.

"And I'm getting mightily hard."

She smiled.

"Unfortunately, I have to use the bathroom first."

She waited for him patiently, snuggling up beneath the sheets thanking all the Lords above for the gift they had given her just weeks before Christmas. "Please let him be the one," she whispered against the pillow that had witnessed so many of her dreams both awake and asleep. "He *feels* like the one, he really does."

She laughed when he dove back into bed abruptly, then she screeched and giggled in protest as he flung the sheets away and leapt on top of her growling. She spread her legs, slipping her arms around his neck as he rested comfortably against her, supporting himself on his elbows.

He looked seriously into her eyes again. "Something is happening here, Miranda."

Whole poems of words welled up from her heart into her throat, but she didn't dare voice any of them. He had joked about being trapped, but the mere echo of the word kept her carefully silent.

"What are you thinking?" he demanded, pinning her down in every possible way.

"I don't know…"

"Yes, you do," he whispered, planting his lips against hers briefly as if he could taste the reply she was denying him. "Tell me," he insisted.

"I can't…"

"Why not?" His cock was growing prominently hard against her soft belly.

"What do *you* think is happening?" she countered desperately.

His smile approved of her defiance, and there was something almost grimly hard about it that turned her on, making her even more aware of how empty her pussy felt waiting to be soothed by his hard cock. Already she was addicted to the unique injection of his thrusts. After just one night she was as helpless as a junkie. She was his slave, his whore, whatever he wanted.

He kissed her lips again whispering, "Would you like me to fuck you?"

This at least was a question she could answer without worrying it might scare him away. "Yes…"

"Yes *what*?"

"I want you to fuck me, Michael."

He pushed himself up, and she couldn't help admiring the strength of his arms as he filled the mouth of her sex with the pacifier of his cock head, her hole crying silently around the tip of his erection for more; for all of him. She needed him as she needed nothing else on earth. She wanted him forever; today and tomorrow and the next day were not enough.

She moaned as he filled her with him slowly, holding her eyes, letting her see how much his erection savored the clinging wet kiss of her pussy opening up for him, and the pain in her soul at the mere thought of losing him mingled with the physical fulfillment in a near agony of pleasure.

"Do you like the feel of my cock in your pussy, baby?"

"Oh yes!"

"You're thinking you always want me inside you, aren't you, Miranda?" He thrust hard, ramming his cock all the way up inside her, forcing her to cry out and arch her back from the glorious shock.

"Oh God!" She closed her eyes.

"Look at me."

Of course she obeyed him, she *wanted* to obey him; she had no choice.

"You're mine, Miranda, do you understand me?"

"Oh Michael!"

"Say it. I want to hear you *say* it."

"I'm yours, Michael! I *want* to be! I... I..."

"It's all right, don't be afraid, just tell me..."

"I love you!" she gasped. "I can't help it, I already love you!" Tears filled her eyes, warm and wet as her pussy. It was utterly terrifying because it was so absolutely enlightening as for the first time her flesh and her feelings crossed a mysterious horizon and became breathtakingly one.

He rolled over onto his side, pulling her with him and lifting one of her legs over his hips so his erection remained buried deep inside her. "I'm falling in love with you, too, Miranda."

* * *

The power went out right after they finished wolfing down breakfast. The overhead light in the kitchen flickered a few times in warning, then died.

"Good thing your heat isn't electric," he commented, draining his second cup of tea.

"And I have a gas stove, too, and plenty of candles."

"This is going to be cozy."

"Are you being sarcastic?" she asked defensively.

"Not at all. Why would you think that?"

"I don't know..." She looked away, vaguely ashamed. "I guess I'm just used to it. Being flippant, detached and sarcastic seems to be what's considered cool these days."

"I'm going to get angry, Miranda, if you keep confusing me with most people."

"I'm sorry." She smiled at him.

"Or do you just love me for my looks?"

"*Oh please.*"

"Doesn't feel very good, does it."

"Sorry, Michael, I really am, it's just… I can't quite believe you're real!"

"I've done my best, tried my absolute hardest, to convince you of how real I am, Miranda, nevertheless, I'll take that as a compliment."

She pushed her chair away from the table, craving the normalcy of efficiency in the face of so much breathtaking intimacy. "I'll clean up."

He stood up. "*We'll* clean up."

He helped her stock the dirty plates and cups in the deep porcelain sink. "You know, Miranda, there's a lot you don't know about me," he warned. "I'm not as wonderful as you think."

"Yes you are," she said firmly. "We all have our faults and our quirks, but that doesn't affect the quality of our soul."

He turned on the hot water.

"Oh no, Michael, you don't have to do this."

He squirted so much of the concentrated dishwashing detergent onto the sponge that dozens of tiny bubbles caught the dim light from the window and wafted perfect little prisms around them. "I know I don't have to do anything," he spoke almost sternly, "I *want* to do this for you, Miranda."

"Thank you."

"That was the most delicious breakfast I've had in a long time."

She watched him attack the dirty dishes with an efficient energy that, like everything else about him, aroused her and made her feel safe all at the same time. It made her feel she was truly in the right hands at last.

"I never knew a vegetable omelet could taste so good," he added.

"It was the smoked provolone cheese I put in it," she admitted.

"Whatever. It was fabulous."

She leaned against the counter, standing as close to him as possible with-

out interfering with his movements, watching the muscles in his bare arms flex as he scrubbed, rinsed, and placed the dishes on the other side of the sink to dry. "Aren't you cold?" she asked.

"I'm fine."

Well, *she* certainly didn't have a problem with him wearing just his jeans. "So you grew up in Dorchester," she confirmed, feeling compelled to make conversation.

"That's right."

"And your parents still live there?"

"Yes, but my dad and I aren't on speaking terms right now."

"I'm sorry."

"He'll come around. Either that or I'll realize he was right. But enough about me. This seems like the perfect day for you to read me some of your poetry."

"Okay," she agreed timidly.

"Go light some candles in the living room and turn up the heat. I want you to read to me naked."

* * *

Miranda's Poems*

I
I want to be where I cannot tell
the darkness from his skin, it
would feel the same and never end.
Where no responsibility of light
separates our eyes. We would look

into a house at night, at a desk
by the window. Our bloodstains
would still be there under the
lamp left on.

II
I saw stars in the grass, exclamation points
answered with dirt. But a lamp reflected against
the sunset is the memory of flesh after its death.
At night he is a section of the sky looking down.
My hair is lashes that keep the dirt from him so
that he remains open somewhere. The atmosphere
doubles a star. I telescope from here to there
in thought, but I know there is no distance between us. The brain is a fish out of mystery.
Eternity is buried in the smooth ground of the
palm, the lifeline is the root into it.

III
The pure blue of the sky
is darkness thinned by life.
The yard is planted inside
the black and white picture
by the glass frame, made
for shattering.

IV
I pass the lighthouse while my

eyes drown in the formations of a
body. Death burns the corners of
your card, chars the game away.
A black river into which the
color streams flow, veins from
thought to nourish the darkness
of flowering.

V

Like a cat for a lap of darkness.
Piano keys are marble slabs and black
coffins, dark notes made from the
branches of dead family trees. His
lips would be the haunted twist in
the garden of a forgotten Manner.
How in one mouth everything can be
buried, how it can know, a perfected
row of headstones.

VI

A shirt of humid grey air,
buttons of stone. But at
night its folds look like
dark roads I can follow
through him.

MOON DINNER

I was served a half moon for dinner. I pinched it with
my fork and it gave like flesh. Its light streamed onto
the plate. I waited but it did not seem to cool. The
wine was dissolved starlight, vintage red giants. It took
many worlds to fill one bottle, but they still burned, and
in my blood would give the life they had been denied. My
host knew that I cared for the moon, so he usurped the
night and wore a white scarf about his neck like the mist
around a grave. I ate her and drank the stars. There was
a universe more to be had and I discovered that this
eternity is like a dark cellar, created for the feeling it
produces. Lives glow in the dark only waiting their turn.
This wearies me. What happened to the moon? I lie back
on a couch, comforting black drapes around me, as though
the universe folds in and there is time to contain it in
the wound cords that give them the shape of a woman's body.
The moon is in me, I feel her warmth divided again in my
legs, luxuriating in the black dress as though it were the
night itself returned to her. Now he is in a white shirt
that could be land reflecting the inside of me. He is
approaching me, made of light too. But I do not feel him.
There is only a pale countenance in a dark corner of the
room. He is dead and the other half is not here.

*Miranda's Poems are taken from *Fragments For A Papyrus* by Maria Isabel Pita.

* * *

Michael walked behind her where she perched naked on the edge of her ottoman holding the sheaf of papers in her hands. He gathered up her hair and draped it over one of her shoulders so he could begin giving her a neck rub.

"Those are rather dark for a beautiful twenty-three-year-old girl," he said at last, "but I like them. I really do. They're very interesting, and arresting. Thank you for reading them to me."

"Do you like them? Really?"

"If I didn't like them," he dug his thumbs harshly into the tender flesh between her shoulder blades, "I wouldn't say I did. I'm not a liar."

"I didn't mean to imply-"

"You might not have meant to, but it's what you did."

"I'm sorry, Michael, I keep underestimating you."

"Yes, you do. You'll just have to try harder not to in the future."

In the future... The words triggered a purring mechanism deep in her being that should have been audible to him; she was amazed it wasn't, and yet maybe it was, subliminally. He was massaging her so skillfully she had to let her poems fall to the floor as she straightened her back, surrendering to the excruciating pleasure of his thumbs digging deep into her skin.

"Did someone you know kill themselves, Miranda?" he asked gently.

"Yes. He was my boyfriend for a while in high school, but we had broken up months before it happened."

"That must have been terrible."

"He talked about it all the time, it shouldn't have been a surprise, but it was. I didn't believe he'd ever really do it, you know? It was obvious he was unhappy, I felt unhappy that way a lot myself, but… I would never kill myself."

"I understand, you don't have to explain."

"I write about death, but I'm not morbid, Michael, I'm into the mystery of it all. I mean, it's amazing we have a body that can think and feel the way it does, that can touch and smell and desire. Wondering where it came from, and what happens to our sense of self when the brain shuts down, is the ultimate mystery, in my opinion. Some scientists say near death experiences are just the final synapses firing in our neurons, and that what people think they actually experience is happening inside them, not outside in actual reality. But what if inside and outside are the same really? Electricity doesn't need wires to exist, and maybe the spirit doesn't need our veins either but only mysteriously uses them."

"That makes sense."

How casually he agreed with her fantastic reasoning filled her with joy. "I think the eternal energy we're composed of created the body so it could experience itself, it doesn't depend on it to be."

"Maybe it did, and maybe it doesn't, but maybe it's a combination of both."

"Oh yes!" This was a revelation to her. "And that's why it's all so hauntingly complex, because the spirit needs all the laws of manifestation to experience itself the way we're doing now, so that even though it's beyond them it's also, in a sense, forever creating itself through them…"

"I want you to suck my cock, Miranda." He walked around the ottoman to face her, unzipping his pants. He wasn't wearing underwear. He quickly pulled out his penis and slipped it between her lips.

She willingly opened her mouth and let his stiffening length slide down her tongue even though oral sex had never quite worked out for her. She had sucked a handful of her boyfriends down because she felt obliged to do so, but she had never enjoyed the taste of their semen, much less allowed them to ejaculate in her mouth. She wasn't surprised the experience felt very different with Michael from the instant she tasted his dick. The flavor of his pre-cum didn't make her squeeze her eyes shut in distaste, on the contrary, it was so mild, so mysteriously healthy, she found herself eagerly pumping his cock and hungrily twirling her tongue around his head, actively seeking the evidence of his pleasure.

"You're trying too hard," he scolded her mildly. "Relax. Trust me, it feels wonderful."

She strove to obey him by forgetting everything she had read about giving head and by making an effort to just do what she felt like doing. She was curious about the cool fullness of his scrotum, so she cupped his balls in her left hand, caressing them gently as she slipped the tight ring of her lips slowly up and down his full length, reaching up with her other hand to caress his firm stomach.

"Mm, yes," he murmured.

She reached blindly for his hands and placed them on her head, wanting him to use her.

He wove his fingers possessively through her hair. "Let me know if it's too much," he said quietly. "I don't want to hurt you."

She emptied her mouth of his cock just long enough to say, "You won't! I *want* you come in my mouth. Please…"

"Are you sure?"

"Yes. I've never wanted a man to come in my mouth before, this is the first time."

"But it definitely won't be the last." He shoved his jeans down to his knees, then he gripped her head again with both hands and began fucking her mouth the way he really wanted to, grazing her throat with his head.

Bracing herself on his thighs, she moaned and moaned, but not in protest.

Chapter Ten

Sarah's fingers dug deep into the ball of dough she was kneading. Miranda sat at the kitchen table, chin in hands, watching in a contented trance. Her friend's necklaces shone the same colors as the ornaments they would soon be hanging on the Christmas tree Michael was delivering. She hadn't asked him to; he had offered to buy her a tree himself, and this would make its luminous presence in her home even more special.

"How long do you have to keep kneading it like that?" she asked lazily.

"A *fucking* long time!" Sarah replied breathlessly.

"Can I help?"

"No, thanks, I find it quite soothing being able to take out all my frustrations on this helpless ball of dough… I was just reading that *Discover* article in your bathroom. Don't worry, I washed my hands. Do you really think there's such a thing as a God gene?"

"It's fascinating, isn't it?" Miranda sat up, unconsciously crossing her hands in her lap; for her, interesting conversations were a very real form of prayer.

"I've read other articles recently," Sarah continued, "postulating the theory that certain people believe in God, or feel mystically at one with the universe, because they're biologically pre-disposed to. I think that's depressing, not fascinating. It means, Miranda, that the deep down feeling you say you have that your soul is immortal is only a neurological quirk."

"No it doesn't mean that! What came first, the chicken or the egg? Maybe the soul, before it enters the body, programs its own mysterious neurological software according to how developed it is, or what it's goals for that life are. The point is, you know I don't believe the brain causes consciousness. I believe the mystery of consciousness itself fashioned the brain just like we build computers and their software. We use them, but we don't die when we shut them off!"

"You're saying our brains work the way they do," Sarah kept her voice neutral in contrast to her friend's passionate ringing tones, channeling all her emotions into kneading the dough, "because there *is* another so-called higher reality out there we're supposed to sense just like our eyes are designed to register light and our ears sound?"

"Yes, something like that… you have really strong arms, Sarah. I could never do that for so long. I'd love to get a bread machine."

"Oh but that would not be the same at all, *shame* on you. The bread must be seasoned by your salty sweat and your tears of profound boredom to really taste good."

"Right! The few times I've tried baking, I'm pretty sure I killed the yeast. I think my water was too hot."

"If it was as hot as your love life lately," Sarah wiped her brow with the back of her hand, "I'm sure you *fried* the suckers." She gazed sternly at her friend, letting the dough rest. "You're seriously in love with this guy, aren't you?"

"Yes, you know I am."

"Is he in love with you?"

Miranda stood up. "He hasn't said *I love you* again since that first morning, if that's what you mean." She picked up the basket of dirty laundry she had been avoiding. "But he says in the *future* all the time, so there's definitely hope. I'll be right back."

"And I'll still be here slaving over this damn loaf. Was it really my idea to bake fresh bread for Christmas Eve?"

"Yep!"

"Well, next time I have such a brilliant idea, please feel free to talk me out of it."

"It'll be worth it." She twisted the doorknob open without setting the basket down and closed the door with her foot, performing her much rehearsed little laundry dance more gracefully than ever today because she was so happy. Not since she was a little girl had a Christmas Eve felt so special and full of promise. The thrill of unwrapping the big doll's house she had desperately wanted couldn't begin to compare with the excitement of watching a future with Michael opening up before her, gradually and wonderfully unwrapped day by day and night by night. They had only been together two weeks, yet it felt like two months at least judging by the degree of intimacy they had achieved, yet it might only have been two days looking back on all that had happened between them so fast.

For a few days after that glorious snow storm, her pussy was actually a little sore from how often they made love. She had suffered a warm, deeply wonderful ache between her legs she wouldn't have traded for anything. Even the muscles of her inner thighs still hurt in a delicious way, and other muscles she had never even been aware of kept getting her attention with a strangely sweet, silent musical strain from Michael fucking her everywhere and anywhere the mood struck him. She had bent over, precariously poised on tiptoe in the shower, bracing herself on the slippery tiles with her fingertips as he took her from behind, ramming his soap-slick cock into her cunt with such force she was afraid the neighbors would complain about the noise, because she found it impossible not to cry out beneath his thrusts when they were so demandingly deep. He didn't always fuck her that hard. Sometimes he moved slowly in and out of her, fulfilling her in a gentler way when he told her to touch herself, and she obediently climaxed around his excruciatingly patient penetrations.

Bracing the plastic violet hamper on one hip, she walked quickly down the cramped stairwell praying at least one of the machines was available. The landlady didn't charge her tenants to use the facilities, probably because they were so old she had forgotten them. It was so cold and bleak in the laundry room, Miranda thought of it as a subterranean cave containing an old shrine from decades past in which she exercised all her Zen powers of gratitude, determination and patience – she was intensely grateful if there was a washer available when she made the pilgrimage down into the dark bowels of the building, and then her sheer determination to get the tedious chore over and done with seemed to be all that kept the decrepit machine shuddering in the throes of a cleansing orgasm, after which she was forced to exercise the virtue of patience waiting for her clothes to dry, a process that usually took over two hours.

"Oh wow!" She paused in the doorway, grinning in disbelief. All the driers were quiet and empty, which meant the washers were probably all available, too. It was a minor miracle that felt worthy of this already blessed Christmas Eve, the first she was spending with her soul mate...

Her smile vanished as she mentally scolded herself for always thinking of him like that. Sarah was right, she had to leave room for a healthy amount of doubt or she could be seriously hurt if it didn't work out between them in the end; if they broke up, for whatever reason.

She set the hamper down and lifted the lid of a washer, but then she just stood there staring down into the metal and plastic whirlpool, deep in thought. Dimming her present joy in order to theoretically avoid future pain was stupid. If she and Michael broke up, she would be hurt and disappointed and sad no matter what she tried to think about their relationship now. There was no point trying to force a detached, realistic armor over her ideally passionate feelings, it only made her feel stiff and awkward around herself, and around him. Whatever was meant to happen would happen, she decided, energetically feeding handfuls of dirty clothes into the machine's gaping maw, in the meantime, she was going to enjoy, not worry about, how happy being with him, and cherishing her hopes for their future together, made her.

She placed her empty laundry basket on top of the machine and was turning to go when the door opened.

"Patrick!" she gasped, his sudden, completely unexpected appearance startling her to the point of fright. A gust of cold air preceded him into the room that made her shiver, but a much more dangerous tremor shook her deep inside at the sight of his tall and powerful silhouette in a long black leather coat filling the doorway.

He stared at her, surprise combined with a host of other emotions igniting in his eyes so they looked more silver than gray in the dim light, wolf-like… "Miranda…" His voice was barely audible, as if he was struggling not to touch even the syllables of her name.

She had believed – she had convinced herself – she was never going to see him again even though she knew perfectly well that was impossible. Yet she hadn't seen him, or even much thought of him, for two weeks; she had believed she was safe, that she could bury this dirty little secret of hers and Michael would never find out. "How are you?" she asked quietly, raising the plastic bottle of laundry detergent against her chest and embracing it like a baby, vainly seeking to hide as much of her body from him as possible. She was wearing tight black leggings without any panties, and she was suddenly self-consciously aware of how they clung to her labia. She fervently hoped her black sweatshirt was just long enough to conceal the heart shaped space where her inner thighs curved up into her pudenda, which was even more well defined these days by how often the lips of her sex bloomed open around a hard cock.

"I'm fine." His indifferent response did not match the fierce way his eyes were staring into hers.

It was not lost on Miranda that she was reacting like helpless prey by standing there rooted to the spot, yet there wasn't much else she could do since he was blocking her way out. She wanted to tell him she had a boyfriend now, that she was in love, that what had happened between them twice could never happen a third or any other time, but it was impossible for her to say any of these things. She could only pray he felt the same way. The fact that he hadn't been up to see her for two weeks was a good sign that, in his mind, it was also over between them.

"Well," she took a step towards him and the doorway hoping he would react by moving aside politely, "my friend's upstairs baking bread and waiting for me…"

He didn't move.

"You shouldn't be working on Christmas Eve," she heard herself scold him, as if she cared… and maybe she did, she certainly didn't dislike him, she had made that clear enough on more than one occasion…

"It would be hard to keep the Christmas spirit if you froze to death."

"That's true…" He was a dark angel devoted to keeping everyone warm, sacrificing himself for their sakes… she blinked… he was a devil pumping oil straight up out of hell to tempt her against herself and her love on the most holy of days… She let her gaze fall from his eyes to the black leather gloves concealing his hands, gloves that would leave no incriminating fingerprints on her naked body…

He finally stepped into the room and closed the door behind him. "Would you like to watch me fill the tanks, Miranda?" he asked quietly.

"Um… I…"

"Come on, you'll like it." He wrested the laundry detergent out of her hands and set it down next to her hamper on the vibrating washer.

"But my friend-"

"It'll only take a few minutes." He clutched her arm and led her to the small door at the back of the room, keeping firm hold of her as he fished a set of keys from his coat and unlocked it.

"Patrick, I have to go, my friend's waiting," she insisted, making an effort to free her arm from his grip. She couldn't help it if she was both thrilled and terrified by the fact that her half-hearted struggle had no effect whatsoever on the vice-like strength of his black leather fingers. In a flash she realized that if he was wearing wool gloves and another coat of a different material and color that she would not be where she was now, walking down a narrow flight of steps she could barely see in the dim light from a naked bulb hanging in a cold, dank basement in which lay the huge golden dragon eggs of the heating oil tanks.

When the rubber soles of her slipper-socks touched bottom, she felt electrified by a rush of fear and disbelief that numbed her into an almost comfortable sense of denial. He walked past her, and for a few moments she was convinced she was only imagining his ulterior motives and waited calmly for him to open another small door leading outside to his truck. He really *was* just going to show her how he pumped oil into the tanks with his long thick rubber hose…

She tried to forget that the door at the top of the stairs had locked behind them when in fact he did not open the door leading outside and go about his proper business. His black-clad body merged sinisterly with the darkness at the far end of the room, filled with the loud purring of all the radiators in the building working overtime, intensifying the illusion of a vast black dragon coiled around her precious eggs… She wrapped a haunting sense of enchantment around herself to justify the cold stone floor she was for some reason standing on, her arms wrapped protectively around herself as she waited to see what his intentions truly were. She knew his name, he had fucked her twice before, but he was still essentially a stranger and, more importantly, she was in love with someone else, someone who already meant more to her than anything, yet here she was alone with another man. It wasn't possible, she had to be under a spell… the spell of his black leather coat, gloves and boots, and the silver, knife-like glint in his eyes as he strode back towards her, and scooped her body effortlessly up in his arms. He freed her from the gravity of morality as her body relaxed submissively against his chest; lifting her above any responsibility for what was happening. He was her daddy cradling her against him, so strong, so sure of what she needed even though the thought of losing Michael terrified her, lashing her with guilt and shame even while deep between her legs this pain alchemized into an excitement impossible for her to resist.

He set her down at the very back of the room where she could see only the light in his eyes. His leather coat was the cold darkness embodied, all the menacing shadows taken form as she slid her hands down his chest, unable to resist him. His appearance and his actions were pushing all those mysterious buttons in her libido. She was so turned on that the thought of consequences all burned away the instant she considered them. Moths were drawn to the light. She was drawn to the dark, to its all-consuming power as it yanked her leggings down in one fierce motion like an undertow, exposing the warm, wet depths of her sex to the stimulatingly chilly kiss of air trapped underground.

She moaned in real protest as rough wood scraped her naked ass when he lifted her onto a shelf behind her. Her ankles were bound by her leggings; he could only force her thighs open so far, and she made another small helpless sound looking down at his black leather fingers digging into her skin, smooth and faintly luminous as moonlight threatened by his engulfing black cloud. She bit her lip as he reached into the open folds of his coat, and unzipped his pants. He wasn't even going to kiss her. He was simply going to fuck her without saying a word, without even needing to, and she couldn't believe how much the forceful way he took command of her body aroused her. He knew she really didn't want to get away. He knew she was wet for him. He knew this dark secret about her, and because he was the only one who had discovered it in her, she slipped her arms around his neck gratefully. She couldn't wrap her legs around him bound as they were at the ankles by her leggings, and the angle was nearly impossible; he could only get the head of his erection inside her. Groaning in frustration, he gripped her hips, bent his knees, and rammed his full length up into her body.

Her cries were utterly ignored by the rumbling darkness. He was rending her open around him, driving into her harder and harder, and how absolutely his cock filled her up indirectly but relentlessly stimulated her clitoris, which was inevitably responding and dissolving the discomfort; it began flowing away on her lubricating juices, becoming a much sharper and deeper pleasure, the dimensions of his swelling erection roughly caressing her clit from the inside in a devastating way.

"Oh yeah…" He bent his knees a little more and thrust himself all the way up inside her despite the angle. The edge of the shelf sliced into her defenseless ass, her hips painfully trapped in his gloved fingers as they branded themselves coldly into her flesh. All she could do was brace herself on the slippery collar of his coat as he stabbed her with his cock until she was begging for him to come, until she was sure he was never going to come, until she felt he would never stop fucking her, until she never wanted him to stop, not ever, not until her burning clit went novae in the dark space and blew her mind as all the elements composing her flesh mysteriously collapsed into the core of her pelvis, the rumbling of the oil heaters echoing the Big Bang their bodies were worshipping together in a cold dark Boston basement…

"Jesus!" He slipped out of her.

She kept hold of his coat so as not to plunge forward off the shelf and lose her balance.

"Miranda…"

"Don't!" she said, afraid he was going to apologize and transform back into a caring mortal man she should have had the willpower to resist. "Don't say anything, please."

He lifted her off the shelf, then bent down to pull her leggings slowly back up her legs, savoring the task. She didn't help him, shivering with perverse pleasure beneath the impersonal caress of his gloved hands. Her eyes were closed; she wasn't expecting the sudden melting sensation of his warm lips kissing her clit. She cried out louder than ever, reaching behind her to brace herself on the shelf.

"Oh my God, stop, please!" she begged as he tongued her body's glowing seed; it felt positively radioactive, mere seconds away from another complete meltdown. She was embarrassingly aware of her cunt full of his spunk beginning to trickle down the insides of her thighs, until he abruptly plugged her up again, this time with two slick gloved fingers that slipped so effortlessly inside her he immediately added another.

"Oh yes! Yes!" she gasped, gripping the shelf and resisting the urge to brace herself on his head. She didn't want to feel how soft his hair was against his skull, she wanted no reminders of his individual mortality; her orgasm was riding the wave of his intensely violent anonymity. It was breathtakingly easy for her to come again as he finger fucked her, circling the firm tip of his tongue teasingly around her clit before suddenly sucking on it like a candy that dissolved with blinding sweetness in his mouth. But it wasn't enough for him. He kept her crying out for mercy and for more by slipping a fourth finger into her drenched hole, shoving them all the way inside her until he was almost fisting her and making her feel that he could, until she longed for him to thrust his thumb inside her too and beat her to a higher life as she climaxed again...

He straightened up, yanking her leggings up with him and covering the hot wet evidence of her three orgasms with their black cotton bandage. She clung to his coat again, her knees weak. The smoldering warmth in her womb would have seriously frightened her if she hadn't been on the pill, and it still made her nervous. "We can't see each other again, Patrick," she said faintly as he zipped his pants closed. "This was the last time."

"That's what I told myself two weeks ago, and look what happened."

"I know, but this time it has to be. I'm... I'm seeing someone, and he can't find out about this, please."

"It's all right." He took her hand and led her quickly back towards the stairs and the light. "The last thing I want to do is hurt you, Miranda. No one will ever know about us." He turned and tilted her face up to his with both hands, staring down into her eyes, and she wondered if he could see how the caress of his black leather gloves affected her even when she couldn't even think of having another orgasm for a while. "I swear I won't tell anyone if you don't." He kissed her hard but briefly, without opening his mouth, like in an old movie.

"You know I wont, but you have to promise me this is the last time, Patrick, that… that you won't come over again one night when… when I'm not alone…"

He let go of her and stepped back, already turning away as he said dismissively, "Get going. Your friend's waiting for you."

"Patrick, please…"

"Don't worry, Miranda."

"But if you show up and he's there he'll know…"

He strode back towards her and grabbed her arms. "Who is he anyway? Who is this guy you're so fucking in love with all of a sudden?"

"His name is Michael. He's an art student. You know what I do for a living…"

"Yes." He let go of her. "You stand naked in front of complete strangers for money."

The tone of his voice affected her like a blow. She stared at him for a stunned moment, then turned and ran up the steps. She didn't stop running until she reached her apartment and slammed the door closed, locking it furiously behind her.

"What the hell took you so long?" Sarah asked, walking out of the kitchen, her arms up to her elbows dusted ghostly white with flour. "What's the matter? What happened?"

"Nothing!" Miranda sobbed. "Nothing!" She ran into the bathroom and slammed that door behind her, too.

Chapter Eleven

"Are you going to tell me what happened now?" Sarah asked gently, sitting on the edge of the bed beside Miranda where she lay curled up in a ball, but at least the sound of sobbing was no longer emanating from beneath the fiery blanket of hair veiling her face.

Sarah was torn between impatience and concern. She knew a girl could get into trouble doing laundry alone in the basement, but she also knew (or at least she hoped) her friend would have had the sense to call the police right away if that was the case.

"I saw Patrick..." The muffled voice confessed at last.

"You just had sex with Patrick in the laundry room?"

"No, in the basement."

"Ah... he lured you down into his domain!"

She rolled onto her back and looked up at the ceiling, crossing her hands over her womb like an effigy on a tomb, her face pale and hard.

Sarah kept her voice calm, "He didn't rape you, did he, Miranda?"

"Yes, in a way he did, but I let him."

"If you *let* him then he didn't rape you!"

"I'm not so sure about that, but it doesn't even matter." Her voice was listless. "The point is it happened, and I can't believe it."

"*Why* can't you believe it? That's what I don't get. You fucked him twice before, didn't you?"

"That was *before* I met Michael, Sarah."

"Oh so now you're feeling guilty, but that wasn't what you were feeling down in the basement, was it."

"Michael will find out, I know he will, and he'll leave me."

"Oh stop it! You think a married man is going to tell on you? No one's going to find out unless you're stupid enough to let guilt ruin everything and drive you to confess your so-called sins yourself."

"But that's just it, Sarah." She finally looked at her. "How can I possibly keep this, or any other, secret from him when I love him and I want him to know everything about me and want to tell him everything? How can I hide something like this from him forever?"

"You've only been dating him for two weeks, Miranda, he hasn't asked you to marry him yet or anything. For all you know he's still seeing someone else on the side and-"

She sat up, anger blazing color back into her cheeks. "He's *not* fucking someone else on the side! I would know! And he's not like that, he would tell me if our relationship wasn't exclusive! You don't know him like I do, Sarah, but you have to believe me, it's very, very special between us!"

"I believe you," she said soothingly, and then literally had to bite her tongue to keep from voicing her thoughts. *Just like he'll magically know you're cheating on him. Just like you're gong to tell him.*

"Oh God, Sarah, what am I going to do?" She bent her knees and rested her forehead on them, desperately hugging herself.

"Do you realize how lucky you are that every hot man you meet wants to fuck you?" She stood up in an effort to control her anger, but the words hemorrhaged out of her as she worried some beads as if they were a gaudy rosary. "You just had what I get the feeling was really great sex, and yet you're sitting here crying because you were unfaithful to a guy you only met two weeks ago. Okay, so he's bringing you a Christmas tree, but that doesn't mean you belong exclusively to him yet, does it? You're not *married* yet, are you? You're twenty-three-years-old and beautiful. Enjoy it! I know *I* would if I could."

Miranda stared up at her, wide-eyed.

"I'm sorry," she dropped into the chair behind her, "but sometimes it drives me crazy the way you turn how incredibly lucky you are into a curse! That damn Catholic guilt of yours is a real killer. You're young and gorgeous and having the kind of fun most girls can only dream of, and you feel like crucifying yourself because of it. It seriously pisses me off what a waste that is," she finished wearily.

"Wow..." Miranda turned and sat on the edge of the bed, her hands clenched between her thighs now as she absorbed this sermon like the good Catholic school girl she still was at heart. "You're right, I guess... in a way."

"What do you mean *in a way?* I'm right and that's all there is to it." Sarah pressed her advantage, beginning to hope the evening wasn't going to be a complete bust after all.

"Things aren't so simple." Miranda gazed at her earnestly. "Just because I'm young doesn't mean I'm allowed to be irresponsible and lie to a man I really feel I love."

"You're not lying to him by not telling him something. You also have to be smart. In the future, *if* you stay together, you can excite each other by confessing all your dirty little secrets, but right now it would be really stupid for you to say anything. You might hurt Patrick if you did, then you'd end up feeling guilty about *that*."

"You're right, I just can't ever let it happen again!"

"Now you're behaving a bit more rationally."

"But that's just it, it wasn't rational the effect he had on me, Sarah… It's just the way he looked…"

"Go on…" Sarah sat up again, anticipating another vicarious thrill courtesy of Princess Miranda and the erotic perils she was so fortunate to suffer.

"He was dressed all in black," she went on softly, staring into space seeing again the man and the event that had so devastated her virtuous vision of true love, "a long black leather coat, black boots and black leather gloves…"

"Oh my God, Miranda, you have a kinky streak!" Sarah shrieked. "You have a black leather fetish!"

"No, it's not just the leather, it's how tall and powerful he looked…"

"Oh my God!" Sarah laughed, hooting with delight. "You're a kinky little *bitch*!"

"*I am not,*" she protested, but her eyes were shining with relief and even pleasure at being able to talk to someone about feelings she was only just discovering. "He was so *forceful*, Sarah, I couldn't fight him. I didn't want to."

There was a knock at the door.

Miranda leapt to her feet. "Who is that?! It can't be Michael, he said he wouldn't be here until after five! Oh my God, it can't be-"

"Calm down, I'll get the door." She was more than curious to do so, and more than half hoping it would indeed be the infamous Patrick standing out on the landing. Miranda's description had whet her appetite for the sight of a tall, strongly built man dressed all in black, *black leather* to be precise. She was grinning inside. Who would have thought her fairytale princess friend was a kinky little submissive at heart!

"If it's Michael, tell him I'll be right out, Sarah!" She was already locking herself in the bathroom, the age-old refuge of women everywhere, at least after it replaced the outhouse and water closet. The patriarchal force driving civilization's progress had no idea what it had coming to it when it put bathrooms in houses, a place where women could find sanctuary for hours on end. Perhaps the modern bathroom with its comfortable tub had done more for feminism than anyone thought.

"I'll take care of it, you just try and relax, okay," Sarah said firmly through the bathroom door. "You really haven't done anything wrong, so stop your *Mea Culpa* act and get ready for a fun night. This will be a Christmas Eve you'll never forget, that's for sure. "

Whoever it was out on the landing knocked again, not impatiently, not urgently, but they weren't going away. Glad she had washed all the flour off her hands and arms, she stole a quick glance in the hall mirror, and then wished she hadn't. The contrast between her own facade after staring at Miranda for so long was always a bitter blow. "Mirror mirror on the wall," she mumbled, comforting herself with the sight of her deep cleavage, something at least Miranda didn't possess, not yet anyway, although she probably would in her forties; girls like her were made to age well like fine wines, their slender lines filling out so they were even more sensually attractive later in life.

"I'm coming!" she called sweetly, and opened the door wondering who she would see. Well, it certainly wasn't Patrick standing out in the hallway, nor was it Michael, but she wasn't disappointed. "Hi," she said, putting on her brightest smile.

"Hello," the young Japanese man responded politely, staring over her shoulder clearly hoping to catch a glimpse of the apartment's true occupant. "Is Miranda home?" His voice boasted no foreign accent to speak of; he sounded one-hundred percent USDA approved American even though he certainly didn't look it.

Sarah sighed inwardly. "She's indisposed at the moment. Can *I* help you?"

"I saw this box for her down in the lobby and thought I'd bring it up." He did not extend the said offering.

"That's so nice of you, thank you." She held out her hands, careful to keep her sickly yellow nails facing down.

His dark narrow eyes went blank. He was a fine young animal – smooth white flesh, sinewy muscles and black hair growing sleekly down to his broad shoulders – caught in her sarcastic headlights, unable to escape; to think of a way to give the box to Miranda himself without breaking any relational traffic laws. Sarah decided it would be quite enjoyable looking at him for a while, and he would help take Miranda's mind off forceful older men and beautiful soul mate boyfriends for a few minutes. "Better yet," she lowered her hands, "why don't you come inside and give it to her yourself? She's just in the bathroom. She'll be right out."

His eyes remained blacker than onyx as he failed to reflect her smile. "That's okay," he surrendered the box abruptly, turning away, pride making him look even taller; desirably aristocratic.

"Thanks," she said sourly, and somehow managed not to slam the door on him. He wouldn't have refused Miranda's invitation to come inside. He obviously didn't want his presence in the beautiful girl's home, and how effective he might be able to make it, diluted by another female he had no interest in.

She set the box down indifferently. It was from Miranda's parents and probably full of the kind of goodies *her* father, a high-powered and extremely busy attorney in Washington D.C., never bothered to send his only daughter. He did his best to forget Sarah existed, in fact, and she had to admit he was doing a pretty good job of making her feel she didn't exist herself sometimes. She studiously avoided wondering what her life would be like without her Trust Fund. At least her mother had cared enough to leave her that much before she slit her wrists in the bathtub like a true Roman, trapped into marriage with a wealthy Jew when she was too young to realize what it would do to her.

"It's safe to come out now!" she yelled.

Miranda tentatively opened the bathroom door and peered out. "Who was it?!"

"One of your neighbors. He saw a box for you sitting in the lobby and was kind enough to bring it up." She deliberately didn't mention the fact that he was young and handsome and intriguingly Japanese. Now *that* was a kinky race. She had seen some of the adult cartoons they so masterfully produced, and they were darkly arousing, to say the least. However, she couldn't quite picture Miranda all twisted up in some complex Japanese rope bondage. No, her friend's kinky streak was conventionally Western, an unholy brew cooked up by the Catholic church and the Secret Police and a bunch of other psychological ingredients she wasn't inclined to write out the recipe for.

"A box?" Miranda emerged from her sanctuary. She had washed her face and brushed her hair and applied a little bit of makeup, as if she needed it. She had of course also taken a long hot shower before finally confessing her totally slutty behavior down in the basement. She was wearing a fresh pair of black leggings beneath a soothingly pure white cashmere sweater that clung to her breasts and showed off the gentle hourglass curve of her waist and hips. "Who's it from?"

"Your parents, of course."

She smiled faintly, and Sarah knew what she was thinking. Patrick was probably close to her father's age. "However, its delivery interrupted a very interesting conversation we were having, Miranda." She dropped onto the loveseat because she was tired; she was always tired. "Does Michael have any idea at all how kinky you are?"

"I didn't have any idea myself until now." She sat down beside her.

Sarah turned towards her. "How kinky do you think you are deep down, *really*?"

"I'm not into pain, if that's what you mean," she replied at once, staring out the window at the storm-gray sky.

"But how do you know if you've never tried it?"

"I just know," she insisted, frowning stubbornly.

"There's something you're not telling me, Miranda." She said no more, waiting, confident her friend would bloom open and share everything with her because she couldn't help it; she had such an honest, flower-like soul.

"I was just thinking about the way the shelf down in the basement…" she began very quietly, hesitantly, still trying to understand what exactly she had felt. "I was thinking about the way the edge of the shelf was digging into my ass while he was…"

"Fucking you."

"But that wasn't pain, it was just discomfort…"

"Uh-huh. Has a man ever spanked you, Miranda?"

"No… well, maybe once, but it was just a playful smack."

"Imagine if Patrick had spanked you while he was wearing those black leather gloves, and I mean spanked you hard, Miranda. Do you think you would have liked that?"

Her eyes closed and she slumped lower on the cushion.

"Would you have let him spank you, Miranda?"

"Yes," she whispered, "I think I would have…"

"Do you think you would have liked it if he spanked your bare ass with his cold leather gloves really hard?"

"I don't know… maybe…"

"*Maybe?*"

"*Yes!*" she breathed. "I would have liked it if he spanked me *hard*, really, really hard!"

"*Oh my God!*" Sarah crowed. "I love it! You *deserve* to be spanked, don't you, Miranda, because you're a bad, *bad* girl, aren't you?"

"Yes!" She opened her eyes and they were full of worried wonder as she truly saw herself for the first time. "I *really* am."

Chapter Twelve

Michael and Miranda were sitting as close to each other as possible on the loveseat watching television. Sarah had left about an hour ago and now they had their arms and legs draped over each other in an exquisite confusion of body parts. The little Italian Christmas tree he had brought her stood in a corner approximately three feet tall, it's baby boughs weighed down by colorful Christmas balls, tiny white stars glimmering amidst its green needles. Miranda had turned up the heat. It was Christmas Eve, no time to be worrying about her heating bill. It deeply troubled her (although she was forcing herself not to think about it) that she wasn't quite sure if she now had another very good excuse to conserve energy, or if it wasn't such a bad thing if her tank was soon empty...

Sarah's bread had risen beautifully, and they all enjoyed a small feast of roast chicken and oven-fried potatoes to accompany the soft hot dough and two bottles of Merlot. It pleased or how much Michael relished her cooking. She loved fulfilling his appetites in any way possible, and couldn't understand why feminists would have a problem with that since in the process she was also obviously pleasing herself. Growing and preparing the body's nourishment was a vital part of civilization that could only be looked down on as an inferior pursuit by a culture suffering from an over abundance of food. Michael was also the first guy she had ever dated who truly liked drinking wine and seemed to know a lot about it. He loved beer as well, naturally, and the six-pack of Guinness she had bought him made her smile every time she looked in the refrigerator. She had opened her body and her kitchen and her heart and her mind to him without reservations, without holding anything back, except for the fact that only a few hours ago she had fucked a married man in the basement...

"I'm beginning to think your landlady's really your Fairy Godmother, Miranda," he commented during a commercial break, hitting the mute button on the remote. They were watching *Lonely Planet* on the Travel Channel, adventuring together through the mountains of Turkey littered with ancient ruins villagers used as common household objects, fragments of sacred columns carved with winged dragons given new life as pots for growing herbs and garlic. "I can't believe you get free cable, too."

"Mm."

"You're a charmed creature, Miranda Covington."

"No I'm not." Reluctantly, she claimed her limbs from beneath his and sat up. "I'm flesh and blood and have plenty of faults."

"We all do." He turned his head on the cushion to look at her, the flickering light from the screen silently flashing an SUV commercial caressing his face as if reveling in his ideal bone structure. His hair was disheveled and fell in a golden harvest across his forehead almost into his eyes; it desperately needed trimming. "Is something wrong, Miranda? You seem tense suddenly."

She crossed her arms over her chest and stared at the vision of her Christmas tree, hating herself for ruining the pleasure she could take in it. "I have to tell you something, Michael," she admitted tightly. "I don't want to keep anything from you…"

He sat up alertly, turning his body to face hers. "I'm listening."

She glanced at him. His face looked grave. She was horribly sure he wouldn't just understandingly bury this transgression of hers forever and graciously forgive her. Sarah was right, she was a complete idiot to be doing this, but she had no choice. Her soul was squirming inside her like a cat writhing to get out. Part of her was wild and seriously kinky, she had found that out about herself today, and until she shared this aspect of her personality with him she couldn't relax and be sensually content in his arms again… that is if he still wanted her there…

"Talk to me, Miranda," he urged gently.

Glancing at his face again, the depth of concern in his eyes told her she couldn't possibly take the plunge and tell him everything. She would tell him most of the truth and hope it would be enough to soothe the demons of her guilt. "Right before I met you," she gazed into the shimmering red planet of a Christmas ornament as she spoke, "I had…" She swallowed. "I had an affair with a married man." She closed her eyes.

"I see. Would you care to elaborate on that a little?"

"It wasn't really an affair," she told the darkness, "we never went out, or anything like that… we just slept together three times, that's all."

"Is this man a student in one of the classes you pose for?"

She opened her eyes again but still didn't dare look at him. "No, he's… he's an older man."

"And older men can't be aspiring artists?" he asked impatiently.

She focused on the Christmas tree again even though it's colorful beauty mocked how bleak she suddenly felt inside. "I just needed to tell you, Michael."

His voice softened somewhat, "And I appreciate that."

She caught a glimmer of hope much more precious than the rope of lights putting the young pine in luminous bondage.

"So, where *did* you meet him?"

"Does it matter?" she asked desperately. "It's over."

"It matters to me. I'd like to know."

"I promised him I'd never tell anyone," she braced herself and met his eyes, "but I can't keep any secrets from you, Michael."

"Telling me will be like telling yourself, Miranda, you know that."

"He's the man who delivers the heating oil to the building. One night when it was really cold out he said this was his last stop and I asked him if he wanted some hot tea... I don't know how it happened, it just... happened."

"It's okay." He draped a reassuringly possessive arm over her shoulders, murmuring into her hair, "I'm not judging you, I just wanted to know."

"I've never done anything like that before, Michael," she confessed miserably. "It was just sex, and that's not like me at all..."

"It's okay," he repeated, "now I know, and I'm glad you told me. You say you want to tell me everything about you, and I want to *know* everything about you. I'm even more fascinated by you now than I was a few minutes ago."

She laughed from the intensity of her relief. "Why?"

He whispered, "Because it turns me on what a bad girl you were!"

Her body tensed with an expectation she almost didn't dare indulge, but then she couldn't resist, she heard herself ask him, very softly, almost before she knew what she was saying, "Do you think I deserve to be spanked, Michael?"

He was silent for a long moment. It might only have been her imagination, but she seemed to sense his body grow subliminally heavier against hers, as though the tone of her voice, and what she had said, mysteriously relaxed a part of him he had kept rigidly under control until then. When he finally spoke it was just as carefully and quietly as she had, as if her living room was a confessional sanctified by Christmas Eve, "Do you *want* me to spank you, Miranda?"

She suffered a thrill because she was about to receive a dark gift, a gift her body had secretly wished for without daring to add it to the conscious list of things she desired. "Yes, Michael, I've been a bad girl, I want you to punish me."

He lifted his arm from around her and rose. "Get up," he commanded.

The tone of his voice reached into her very soul. She obeyed him without looking up at his face, she couldn't, she was too shamefully excited.

"In the spirit of not hiding anything from me, Miranda, take all your clothes off, *now*."

In less than thirty seconds she had divested herself of sweater, leggings and socks and stood naked before him gazing down at the rug adorning the wooden floor of her living room. Strangely enough, until that moment she hadn't noticed how sinister it's red and black spiral designs looked, almost like dragons, and her knees literally felt weak as she remembered the roar of the oil heaters down in the basement.

"Now turn around, kneel down, and bend over the cushion," he instructed in that inflexible tone that pulled all her sexual strings as if her body was a marionette helplessly responding to the superior forcefulness of his voice, which seemed to come from a source that was more than who he was as an individual.

She turned around and sank to her knees more reverently than she ever had in church, and then was surprised by how comfortable she felt with her breasts, arms and cheek resting against the loveseat, her ass thrust up in the air waiting for whatever he desired to do with it. She sensed him sink to his knees beside her and braced herself. She reminded herself that she wanted this, and she wanted it to hurt even though she had no idea why.

"Do you know why I'm doing this, Miranda?"

"Yes…"

"Yes *what*?"

"Yes, Michael?"

He passed a hand lightly over the cheeks of her ass, lingering over her crack. "I want you to tell me why I'm doing this."

"Because I'm a bad girl…"

"That's right. And why are you a bad girl?"

"Because… because I had sex with a married man."

"Yes, you did." He slapped her ass hard.

She let out a small cry, but didn't cringe away from the punishment she had, unbelievably enough, asked for herself. It really hurt, much more than she had expected it to.

"Are you ever going to do that again, Miranda?"

"No!" she replied fervently. "I swear I won't, Michael."

He spanked her again.

She couldn't stop herself from letting out an incredulous sob and twisting her hips back and forth in a vain effort to dim the burning afterglow of his blow. There was a sharp, inescapable quality to the pain that took her breath away in disbelief, mainly because she had herself requested its terrible intensity.

"Have you ever been spanked before?" he demanded quietly.

"No, never!"

Maria Isabel Pita

"What do you think so for?" He forced her ass cheeks to quiver beneath another vicious smack before she had a chance to respond. "Does it hurt?"

"Yes!"

"That's good. It's supposed to hurt. How many do you think you should get for being such a bad girl?"

"I don't know!" She seriously didn't think she could take many more.

"I haven't even started, baby." He read her mind.

"Please…"

"Please *what*."

"Not too many, please, Michael."

He subjected her to a fourth blow, this time concentrating on her right cheek.

She wailed in protest and tried to straighten up.

He placed his hand firmly on her upper back and pushed her down. "Stay right where you are," he commanded. "If you try that again or try to cover your ass with your hands you'll only make it worse for yourself. I'll give you three more every time you try and escape what you have coming to you."

Her ability to think froze beneath a cold wave of fear that was also somehow perversely enchanted. Her thoughts seemed to be waiting for a prince to break the spell with a kiss – the dark, painful kiss of his open hand against her defenseless bottom cheeks. Even as she squeezed her eyes shut and whimpered in distress to let him know she couldn't take much more, she was forced to acknowledge to herself that this was something she had been waiting for, secretly longing for, even though at the moment she couldn't even begin to wonder why.

"I'm going to give you ten in a row," he warned, "and each one is going to be a little harder than the last."

She was acquiescently silent as he began spanking her in earnest. She would never have believed remaining submissively motionless would be the most difficult exercise of her life. She found herself thinking it would be easier to run ten miles than to lay still as he punished her with increasing severity. She was astonished by how hard a man's hand could be as it came down repeatedly over the infinitely tender spot where her buttocks flowed down towards her thighs, the combined length of his palm and fingers devastating both her cheeks as he concentrated on hitting her directly over her crack.

One, two, three, four… She counted in her head like an athlete straining to reach the finish line. Clutching the cushion, she turned her head and buried her face in it.

Five, six… She fervently wished he would spank her faster so she could get it over with, but he paused long enough between each blow to allow the pain to radiate even deeper, and sear her flesh in the form of an almost unbearable burning in all her blood cells rushing to the surface of her fine and excruciatingly sensitive skin.

Seven, eight… She was vaguely aware of her muffled sobs and much more acutely, astonishingly conscious of how hot and wet her pussy was becoming. It made no sense at all, but her sex was responding to this violent version of a caress as it never had to the most expert fingers and tongue.

Nine… Just one more excruciating stroke to go of his artist's hand painting her ass a flaming red that was not part of any normal sexual palate. He let his palm hover just a breath away from her tormented cheeks so she could feel it's threat and dread the last, most vicious whack of all for a few torturous seconds.

"Keep still," he said shortly, and Miranda realized she was unconsciously swaying her hips back and forth in an effort to deflect the final slap to a fresh spot on her ass.

The sound of his open hand once more making contact with her screaming skin echoed through the apartment like a deeply buried tectonic plate in her psyche cracking and dividing her life into before she was spanked and after she was spanked by her lover. Nothing would ever be or feel the same again.

"Have you had enough?" He caressed her hot skin, soothing the smoldering ache by gently squeezing each of her cheeks in turn.

Her pores – that had absorbed the hot punishment like a sponge – now let it flow into the rest of her body as a languid peace that made her rest her cheek passively against the cushion as she sighed, "Yes!"

"Yes?" he prompted.

"Yes, Michael, I've had enough… thank you."

"You need to learn how to address me properly, Miranda."

Her thoughts were beginning to thaw and this statement both thrilled and worried her in that doubled edge way she was becoming strangely addicted to. "Yes, Michael."

"We'll work on it."

His hard voice made her even more aware of how ready her pussy was for him. She began to push herself up, and gasped when he planted his hand firmly between her shoulder blades again to hold her down.

"Did I give you permission to move?"

"No… please fuck me, Michael, I'm so wet…"

"Fucking you is hardly a good way to punish you."

"Oh God!" she groaned. This was either the most horrible or the most wonderful Christmas Eve of her life; she suddenly wasn't sure how she felt about it. Her kind, sensitive, considerate lover had transformed into a stern disciplinarian she almost didn't recognize, especially since she couldn't look into his eyes. And against all comfortable odds, earlier that day she experienced some of the best sex of her life down in a cold basement with a man old enough to be her father. These events were strange dark gifts indeed, and she had no idea if the part of the Magic Pattern delivering them to her was good or bad; she wasn't at all sure if she should hold onto them and see where they led her, or if she should return them straightaway before they turned her into damaged goods.

"You're going to stay there just like that for a while," he told her as she felt him rise to his feet behind her. "I want you to think about what a bad girl you were, and about what you felt while I was spanking you. I also want you to think about how you should address me in the future when I'm disciplining you."

In the future, the three magic words that applied a sweet, soothing balm to the ache in her bottom, and to the deeper discomfort in her soul as she wondered what was happening here and whether it was right to embrace it or if she should run for her life. But of course she had no choice, she was in love with the man giving her these commands. She was also astute enough to recognize that, ultimately, it was he who was obeying her desire that he behave this way, and this realization was the key that relaxed her completely.

"Yes, Michael, thank you."

Chapter Thirteen

Miranda spent the first day of the year lost on the Internet seriously questioning the wisdom of her New Year's resolution to explore her kinky side. It was almost impossible to get through the forest of X-rated pop up ads bombarding the mystery of her libido with images that were much too well lit and fixated on faceless organs to turn her on. But she was determined to learn more about the lifestyle she was embarking on rather like Red Riding Hood blithely unaware of the wolf and it's dangerously sharp teeth and claws. Her ass had certainly been red after Michael spanked her, even after she lay bent over the loveseat for a while listening to the soothing sensual scraping of charcoal against paper as he sketched her. Afterwards, he led her naked into the bedroom, turned her around, and made her look at her bottom cheeks in the mirror still blushing from the humiliating punishment she had actually thanked him for.

Only remembering the conversation they had later in bed gave her the courage and determination she needed to navigate the Web trying to find out more about the acronym BDSM. She had always been aware of it, like a distant exotic land on a map too far removed from her world to worry about, a place she had never seriously entertained thoughts of visiting, much less living in. The terrain was frighteningly unfamiliar, the atmosphere darkly sinister, the landscape full of potentially dangerous pitfalls, and yet the very air around her suddenly felt more invigorating than the same oxygen molecules she had been breathing only a few days ago, last year, in another world before she was spanked by the man she loved; before she begged him to punish her and he complied with a forcefulness that obviously came naturally to him.

Lying in each other's arms later that night, he joked about the handcuffs he had "borrowed" from his dad when he was a teenager and that he still had. She giggled, sleepy and contented, not realizing then how much the thought of these handcuffs would begin to obsess her. She pictured them snapping open in his hands, silver crescent moons rising into her mind dozens of times a day, haunting her psyche with fantasies so dark she could scarcely make them out. He wouldn't just handcuff her to the bed and fuck her; he would do a lot more than that to her while she was powerless to resist…

Just what he would do to her she was trying to figure out on the Web, more full of images and information than the ocean was of fish all hopelessly tangled in the virtual net of her search requests. Her soul began to wrinkle its virtual nose at the pornographic stench – so many bodies flopping and surging and writhing meaninglessly together – as her psyche was flooded with opinions and perceptions she didn't have the technical savvy to quickly cut through to reach any actual (although still subjectively slippery) facts about BDSM.

She was no closer to clearly understanding the nature and ramifications of the submissive streak she had discovered in herself. Unlike a physical rash she could ask a doctor to examine, this was a mental and emotional condition there paradoxically seemed no cure for except the pain it made her crave. Yet it wasn't pain she desired so much as the whole experience, the different aspects of which were as subtle as they were obvious like figures in an equation that had to be just right or it wouldn't add up to an irresistible excitement. Black leather, a forceful attitude, the unyielding firmness of a man's will combined with how big and hard his cock was, the command in his voice cutting through her thoughts and mysteriously setting her free as she yielded to his demanding touch and violent thrusts...

Trying to talk to Sarah about it wasn't much help either. Her friend wanted to blame everything on the fact that Miranda had been a Catholic school girl, as well as an only child thoroughly spoiled by parents who never laid a hand on her as punishment. On the face of it, these were perfectly reasonable psychological roots for her kinkiness. If she didn't feel guilty, she wouldn't also feel the need to be punished, and if she had been more disciplined as a child, not always getting her way, she wouldn't feel compelled to be treated more strictly now for her own mysterious good. It all made sense, yet it didn't explain why the sight of Patrick filling the doorway dressed all in black leather had turned her on so much she couldn't resist letting him fuck her even though she was in love with Michael. The roots of her arousal went deeper than her mind and its complex psychological web – they seemed to stretch all the way through the earth itself into the darkness of space alive with metaphysical laws intensely difficult to define and impossible to explain away.

It was after six o'clock when she finally shut off the computer in disgust. It was already dark out, late enough to pour herself a glass of Chardonnay and relax for a while wishing she could light a fire. One thing she was sure of at least – she was not into all the extremes of Sadomasochism. Being tortured with needles and clamps and whatever would never turn her on. Thank God Michael had made it clear he was not, and would never be, into any of that either. She wasn't the first girl he had spanked, and she was glad he was experienced enough to confidently take command of her when she practically begged him to punish her. He admitted to also having used his handcuffs on more than one girl, and even the stab of jealousy she suffered perversely deepened the nervous excitement building up inside her. It was strange, once events conspired to make her recognize the dark nature of her appetites, how hungry she was for more, painfully so. The weekend when she would see Michael again seemed an eternity away, and the strain of waiting for it was aggravated by the fact that she couldn't visualize what might happen when they next saw each other again. What would he do? What did she want him to do? She couldn't stand the thought of nothing at all happening and leaving her feeling even more frustrated, and dangerously disappointed. But if she was submissive to her lover, she couldn't exactly command him to behave a certain way. She wasn't sure herself what she actually desired to experience and suffer.

Tomorrow was only Wednesday and she wouldn't even be seeing him in passing at Mass Art because she was posing in private for a celebrity who had contacted the art department and requested their best model. She wrote down the man's Cambridge address and forgot all about it until now sipping her Chardonnay. He was a musician of some sort, his name had rung a distinct bell, and suddenly she found herself wondering who he was. She probably listened to his music, although it didn't matter if she did or not; he was paying her to be quiet and naked, not to talk. The last thing he probably felt like dealing with was a chatty little groupie, nevertheless, she was curious.

Sitting cross-legged on the carpet, her glass of wine handy, she began sorting through her extensive CD collection. She rarely looked through it; the moment she bought a new one she recorded the whole thing onto her ipod. Somehow she found the band almost at once, the lead singer's name on the back jacket leaping out at her in a slap of bold black letters that made her gasp in shock that she hadn't realized before who he was. The group's name was *Sieve*, and in her mind their main claim to fame was the fact that she had masturbated to their music dozens of times, to one particular track, in fact.

"Oh my God!" she said out loud, laughing and shivering at the same time. She was actually going to take all her clothes off in front of this handsome man who was dressed all in black leather in the picture, a sexy goatee framing his hard mouth... she was going to submissively assume any position he told her to...

She slipped the jacket out of the plastic container and flipped through the pages looking for the lyrics of the song she had climaxed to countless times. When she found them, she forgot all about her Chardonnay, her mouth hanging open in wonder as if an invisible cock had slipped between her lips and was offering her the answer to everything.

Chapter Fourteen

Miranda was glad she never really had to worry about what to wear to work. Her primary concern when dressing was how quickly she could strip naked. Her job was much easier in the summer when she could just slip on a sundress and sandals. Winter complicated things with layers, but when you walked to a bus stop and just stood there for a while, there was no avoiding leggings and T-shirts and everything else she could bundle herself up in.

She dressed entirely in black for her gig in Cambridge. She was posing nude for a rock star; it felt right. Besides, she was into her newfound appreciation for the mysterious power black had over her senses and sensibilities, especially when imbuing handsome, virile men with all the powers of darkness…

A man gave up his seat on the bus for her, so she was able to think in comfort during the ride to the train station. She was glad it hadn't snowed since Christmas Eve and most of the ugly slush had been cleaned from the sidewalks and streets. It was an overcast day, but the forecast did not cause her to worry about her commute home later. She was listening to *Sieve* on her ipod and thinking she should be a little concerned about her growing obsession with the color black, not to mention with dark and powerful forces embodied in men. None of this had anything to do with the real loving relationship she was developing with Michael, and yet it *had* to, somehow; it turned her on too much to give up. Fortunately her young lover seemed more than willing to explore these unorthodox feelings with her, and she was immensely grateful to the Magic Pattern for this. She thanked Fate every morning as she got out of bed. *Please Lords*, she said in her head, *give me health and love.*

It was a relief to get off the bus in which the heat was turned up too high and to walk quickly in the bracing cold down into the subterranean chill of the station. She loved the sight of a train approaching down the dark tunnel, it's lights evoking the fiery face of a dragon cutting through the darkness as it roared swiftly between the platforms like a supernatural serpent all lit up inside with undigested human bodies. Today she was only going two stops to Harvard Station. From there she would catch a cab (an expensive that would be reimbursed her) to the musician's home.

Her driver was a young black man who cheerfully asked her where she was headed.

"To work." She smiled back at him in the rearview mirror and gave him the address.

"To work? At a private house? You're too pretty to be a maid…"

"I'm not."

"Hmm…" He glanced back at her over his shoulder.

"I'm an artist's model," she told him, a little disturbed by what she imagined he was thinking.

"An artist's model? I've never had an *artist's* model in my cab before. What you do exactly?"

"I pose naked."

He laughed. "You get paid just to take your clothes off, girl?"

"Uh-huh."

He laughed again, then was silent for a moment before adding beneath his breath, "We all have to work for a living" as if he didn't believe her.

His attitude didn't help how nervous she was the closer they got to the address scribbled on her pink post-it paper. Judging from his lyrics, Richard Adams was more than superficially acquainted with Bondage & Domination, which made this gig feel potentially much more interesting than she should be allowing it to feel. In light of her recent lack of self-control, this worried her, even though it was highly unlikely he would be wearing black leather in the comfort of his own home in the morning. She sincerely hoped not, because her moral resolve had more than once slipped dangerously on black leather when worn by a handsome, confident man...

"Have fun." The driver dismissed her with a wink.

"You too." She started briskly down a brick path winding between big old trees. The old stone house and carved wooden door were big enough to belong to the annex of a castle invisible in the mist rising from the ground. The sun was high in the sky, but it was colder and darker now than when she left home. She rang the bell and waited for a servant to admit her.

She was caught completely off guard when Richard Adams himself opened the door. "Hi!" she squeaked like a mouse abruptly confronted by a cat. She couldn't believe he was actually dressed entirely in black – a black sweatshirt, black sweat pants, and black slipper-socks. The outfit was casual, but had definitely not been bought at Walmart; the shirt draped over his broad shoulders in a luxurious way that looked custom-made. His sweatpants were not quite as fine, but they were enticingly soft and (she shocked herself by thinking) left plenty of room for his cock to harden and grow. He looked just like he did in the photograph on his CD cover, except that in person his goatee was even more sinister.

"Hello, Miranda." He stepped back. "Come in please."

She walked into the house, and was glad to note the heat wasn't turned up to the point where she would grow uncomfortably drowsy while posing.

He closed the door and stepped behind her. Before she could do it herself, he unwound the scarf from around her neck. "Let me take these." He caressed her hat off her head and, after she hastily unbuttoned it for him, he slipped her coat down her arms .

"Thank you," she said as he hung everything up for her.

"*Thank you* for coming all the way out here. I much prefer working in private than in a crowded classroom."

"Oh, I understand, it's no problem at all."

"Can I get you anything to drink before we begin?"

"No, thank you, I'm fine."

"Well," he rested a hand lightly on her upper back, "come this way then."

Michael's hand had rested right there between her shoulder blades when he pushed her back down against the cushion after spanking her, angry she had moved without his permission...

He led her into a cozy fire-lit parlor that could have been the set of a movie about a wealthy Boston gentleman. The room possessed none of the edgy personality of his music, and she didn't know whether to be relieved or disappointed.

"I'm only renting this place for a few months," he answered her unspoken thoughts.

"Oh…"

"What I want to do today, Miranda," his hand still resting on her back, he guided her over to the fireplace and a rug spread across the gray hearth stones, "is to try and capture the play of light and dark over your body."

"Okay." She hated herself for being stupidly monosyllabic.

He slipped his hands into the pockets of his sweatpants and stood before her, looking her up and down slowly.

She was suddenly afraid he was wishing the department had sent him a different model, someone more interesting to work with, a girl with bigger breasts maybe…

"I'll need you to pose for me completely in the nude, Miranda. Is that all right?"

"Oh yes!" she breathed her relief he wasn't disappointed with her. "That's not a problem at all, I do it all the time." She hated how cheap that made her sound, but she was anxious to assure him he wasn't going to have any issues with her.

"Great." He smiled, his teeth sharply white framed by his black goatee. "Then let's do it. You should be warm enough by the fire." He turned away and walked over to an easel, the only object in the room that didn't appear to belong amidst the burgundy leather wingback chairs, and the heavy mahogany shelves filled from floor to ceiling with old books that looked to her as if the last time they were read was over a century ago.

She began stripping, shutting off her thoughts and feelings by reminding herself this was a job, that he was paying Mass Art good money for her to be here, and that he had no idea whatsoever how much she enjoyed masturbating to one of his songs. She hadn't even told him she listened to his music, or that last night she had finally read the lyrics to the track that turned her on so much, and found out why.

She draped her clothes over the closest chair and set her boots neatly at its feet, keeping her back to him as long as possible, but then there was nothing else for her to do. She turned around to face him praying he would like the figure he had to work with. She gasped, because he was standing just a hand's breath away; he had crossed the room again as silently as a cat.

"I'm sorry, I didn't mean to startle you." He caressed the hair over her shoulders with the backs of his hands. "You have beautiful hair, Miranda, but it hides too much of the rest of you."

"I can pin it up," she offered helpfully, unable to stop herself from staring up at his face. There was something feral about the way he smiled – all those white teeth contained in a thin black frame – that made her catch her breath in a way she couldn't conceal from him.

"No, I want you to keep it down, it's an amazing color, just don't let it cover your breasts."

"Okay… I love your music!" she confessed.

"And you're beautiful, but I'm not a musician today… although I guess in a way I am… there's a silent visual harmony in the lines of the human body, especially a woman's body, that fascinates me." He studied her as he spoke, his dark eyes lingering over all the different parts of her, beginning with her rosy painted toenails and moving slowly back up to her eyes. "I'll never be an artist, but I'm sure I can learn something from trying, and it inspires me." He took her by the hand and led her across the rug to one side of the large stone fireplace crackling with five big logs that would burn for hours. It was the sort of fireplace she dreamed of living with one day, and maybe that's why it felt strangely dream-like when he gently grasped her other hand and genuflected before her as though about to propose. "I want you to kneel right here, Miranda."

She did as he said, his eyes holding hers steadying her with their direct regard.

"Now sit back on your heels," he allowed her hands to slip out of his in a way that immediately made her miss their firm warmth, "and rest your hands on your knees. No, not like that, with your palms facing up... that's it. Beautiful." He stood up. "Are you comfortable like that?"

"Oh yes." She truly was; this was a position she could hold for quite a long time. There was something yoga-like about it that made her feel relaxed and centered in herself. The nervous anxiety she had been suffering began flowing away through her fingertips. The heat was turned down even lower than she had realized, and the contrast between the chilly depths of the dimly lit room to her left, and the warmth of the flames caressing her body on the right, was both soothing and stimulating, so that there was no danger of her becoming drowsy. He stood looking down at her for a few moments, and she was curiously proud of the way her nipples hardened, eagerly responding to the room's contrasting climates, but even more so to the intangible caress of his eyes. She kept her own eyes fixed modestly on the patterns of the rug at his feet, until he didn't move for so long that she finally glanced uncertainly up at his face again.

"Let me know when you need a break, Miranda."

"Okay," she said as he walked away and switched on a lamp that shone a light directly over the canvas perched on the easel. He began by sketching her outlines, his short hair and goatee seeming to grow even blacker as he concentrated, the light gilding one side of his face. She let her eyes linger on the hawk-like quality of his bone structure, entranced by how it all worked together to create a strikingly handsome man with a fine, hooked nose and a thin, hard mouth. His soft dark eyes, and the angular strength of his jaw enhanced by the thin black beard, were contrasts that mysteriously came together in a way that fascinated her. She didn't really care that he was a famous musician, a celebrity, that wasn't why he appeared so regal to her… it was remembering how intensely she had climaxed listening to his music…

"Keep your chin up," he commanded quietly.

She obeyed, and it wasn't long before the familiar trance-like state she invariably fell into when posing began blurring the edges of her vision. There was something about not moving a single muscle for so long that acted as a profound soporific on her mental synapses. Gradually, they ceased flashing superficial thoughts like what she would make for dinner later and when she would go buy her new monthly T-pass. Such concerns flickered like fish on the surface of her brain for a while before she began sinking deeper, relaxing into an inner space where daydreams flowed around her like exotic beautiful mermaids she willingly surrendered her imagination to; gladly drowning reason in weightless depths of fantasies tugging on her with the currents of possible and impossible magically coming together…

"I would very much like to know what you're thinking right now, Miranda."

His quiet voice did not intrude on her reverie but rather slipped easily and naturally into it.

"I was just daydreaming," she replied evasively, shifting her eyes away from him onto a ponderous bookcase.

"About what?" he insisted politely.

She wasn't fooled; she distinctly felt the force of his willpower in the consonants and sensed the demanding depth of his feelings in the vowels. "About you," she was forced to admit.

"What about me?"

She kept her voice as casual as she could manage. "I was thinking about one of your songs."

"I'm honored my musical efforts have the power to conjure such a wonderful expression on your beautiful face, Miranda."

She smiled with pleasure at the compliment.

"Which song?"

"Track four on your new CD…" She was looking at his face again; none of the books on the shelves could ever be as interesting to read. "I was thinking about the lyrics…"

He set down the pencil and selected a tube of paint from a wooden box, turning his face away for a moment, and somehow she felt the firmness of his profile directly between her legs. "You liked them?" he asked.

The careful neutrality of his voice was a warning she chose to ignore. "Yes, I read them last night. I had no idea what you were saying before."

He smiled, squirting shining red acrylic paste onto a palette.

"Oh, I didn't meant it that way!" She realized she had just insulted him. "It's just that before I was too… *overcome* to really hear them."

"So you like to dance?"

"Yes, but that's not what I was doing…"

This time when he looked at her she felt he wasn't just impersonally studying the harmonious lines of her skeleton. If he had asked her what she *was* doing she would have lost her nerve and been too shy to tell him, but he didn't ask her, he simply waited for her to tell him, as if there was no question she would because teasing him was not even remotely an option, so even though she couldn't believe she had put herself in this position, she said, "I was touching myself…"

"Go on." He punctuated the gentle command with a series of vigorous brush strokes.

"That's all…" God, she was definitely a bad, *bad* girl. Sarah would never believe it when she told her about this, and Michael now had the right to spank her really hard, so very, very hard… except that she could never tell him, and her mental and emotional transgression would go forever unpunished…

"Did you come?"

"Yes… and not just once."

"How many times have you had an orgasm listening to my music, Miranda?"

"I don't know… I've lost count."

"That's the best review I've ever gotten of my work. Thank you."

"My pleasure…"

"I'll never be a painter," he declared abruptly, tossing the brush down. "I'm much better with charcoal. It's more dramatic." He took the canvas off the easel and replaced it with a large sketchpad.

She thought about how much Michael loved working with red and black charcoal, and how good he was with it, and guilt caused her to hang her head so she could rest her neck for a second, but mainly so she could attempt to gain some control over herself. She should not be flirting with a client like this; it wasn't professional. She was lucky he didn't seem to mind, but someone else might justly have reported her to the department and gotten her fired, and even though men liked to look at her naked, none of them were going to pay her rent…

"I'm going to let you rest for a minute." His voice unexpectedly came from just above her.

She looked up at him trying not to appear anxious. "Thank you." She accepted the hand he offered to help her up.

"I'd like to sketch you in another position, Miranda. Do you trust me?"

"Of course," she replied truthfully.

"I think you might want to be a little more careful what strange men you trust so soon after meeting them, but you're safe with me. The reason I asked if you trust me is because I want to tie you up."

"What?" she breathed, thinking she couldn't possibly have heard him right.

"I'm going to tie your wrists behind your back, Miranda," he kept firm hold of her hand, "and you're going to kneel in front of this chair, then bend over and rest your cheek on the cushion." He drew her over to the leather chair. "Then I'm also going to bind your ankles together."

Why wasn't she saying anything? Because she trusted him *really*? He wasn't *asking* her if he could do these things to her. Her submissive silence was all the answer he seemed to need. He left her for a moment, and she just stood there looking down at the smooth leather where her cheek would soon be resting, her breasts exposed and her ass thrust even more vulnerably up in the air than the night Michael spanked her, because this time her hands would be tied behind her back and her ankles would also be bound, making it impossible for her to push herself up and get away no matter what he chose to do to her…

Standing behind her again abruptly, he pulled one of her wrists up against the small of her back. "It's all right, don't be afraid…" The voice whispering in her ear seemed a part of her; to be coming from so deep inside her she mysteriously recognized it. "You can trust me, Miranda…" He slipped something cool and silky around her wrist, then gently reached for her other hand and tied them firmly together.

She heard herself ask in a small voice even though it was already too late, "You're only going to sketch me, right?"

"Yes." He rested both hands on her shoulders and gently forced her down onto her knees. "If that's all you really want me to do."

Chapter Fifteen

She's kneeling on the Persian rug, her cheek resting on the cool leather cushion of the wingback chair. Her hands are tied behind her, resting against the small of her back, the silk cloth he used to bind them causing her no discomfort, unless she attempts to free herself, then the knot he made grows tighter, forcing her to hold still. Her ankles are also bound together, her naked ass thrust up in the air. It's not a terrible position even though all she can see is the chair's brass-studded arm. She knows where he is only because she can hear the rough scraping of charcoal against paper. The sound is comforting, it helps her feel safe even though she's completely helpless. His sketching falls into lulling rhythm with the crackling of the fire, the heat of the flames gently caressing her buttocks, the chill air closer to the floor wafting around her dangling breasts hardening her nipples. In contrast his silence is absolute; he says not a word to her as he captures her submissive pose on paper. She doesn't want to be upset that since he tied her up he hasn't touched her. She shouldn't want him to touch her or to do anything else except draw her, yet her pussy begins to feel very differently the longer it remains exposed to teasingly warm gusts from the fire whenever the wind blows harder outside. He doesn't ask her if she needs a break even though it seems like a very long time she's been kneeling there for his insultingly detached pleasure. A single question keeps ringing in her head in rhythm with her heartbeat. How can he resist her? The answer hurts more than her knees starting to complain about the hard stones beneath the rug. She isn't beautiful enough to tempt him. Her body doesn't turn him on enough. It's difficult to think rationally in the utterly defense-less position he put her in. It doesn't help to tell herself she's very fortunate he possesses more self-control than she does. She feels increasingly hurt by his indifference to her highly inviting position. It's not a pose like any she has ever held before. She can't even begin to fall into a trance of fantasies, not when her body is holding the shape of one. Her muscles are smolder-ing gently from the strain of remaining motionless, but it can't compare to the burning indignation in her chest intensifying with every passing minute he remains indifferent to the absolute trust and submission she is offering him. He was right, sketching her is not all she wants him to do, but she can no more admit this than she can free her hands and feet.

Her tormented reverie is intruded upon by a distinct new sound. The door to the room just opened, yet she can still hear the cat-like scratching of charcoal against paper, which means he didn't leave without telling her…

"She looks much better than that," a man's voice she has never heard before remarks.

Her body tenses in disbelief. She is bound naked hand and foot alone in a fire-lit room with two perfect strangers. She must be dreaming. She could not possibly have allowed this to happen…

"She's quite a sight, isn't she?"

She senses the subtle vibration in the floor as the stranger walks across the room towards her.

"Miranda, this is Alex, my very good friend," Richard informs her. "You can trust him, too."

She tries to sound calm. "May I take a break now, please?"

"Not yet. Relax."

His response stuns her. None of the private clients she poses for ever deny her a rest when she requests it. But how silly of her to be shocked by this more than by the fact that none of them have ever tied her up before either.

"Hello, Miranda." Alex's voice comes from directly behind her.

"Hello…" Despite the more obvious heat emanating from the fire she can sense the warmth of his body, and feeling him without being able to see him has a strange, drug-like effect on her…

"You know, Alex, you're just what the picture needed," Richard says casually. "Miranda, I'd like him to kneel behind you, if that's all right."

She can't seem to think straight. The answer should be "No" but she remains silent, in the grip of a debilitating excitement she dreads to even admit to herself. Yet nothing bad has happened; he's keeping his promise and merely sketching her. "I don't know…" The man standing behind her isn't just another model.

A black-gloved hand rises over her face and cold fingertips caress a stray strand of hair away from her eye. "Don't be afraid," Alex urges quietly.

Something melts deep inside her as all her frightened thoughts succumb to a mysterious head rush, the cool sensation of his touch registering as a flash of desire in the warm, wet space between her thighs. "Okay," she whispers.

The slick sensation of a leather coat caresses her ass and the backs of her thighs as he kneels behind her, and the synapses in her brain flicker helplessly she is so turned on; her ability to think rationally extinguished, leaving her feeling dangerously languid.

She discovers another figure in the mysterious equation of her sexual psyche – it deeply thrills her that she knows nothing about the man kneeling so intimately behind her; that she has no idea what he looks like. Her imagination is given free reign, overwhelmingly intensifying the inexplicable yet undeniable power the black leather he's wearing has over her.

He lifts her hair off her neck, and wraps his black-gloved fingers around it gently but firmly.

She closes her eyes. She is not innocently posing with a man while another man sketches them, it can't possibly be all that's happening, her body is reacting too intensely...

Her eyes fly open, shocked by the touch of leather against her mouth as his thumb caresses her lips.

"Suck on it," he whispers.

She moans, but a stab of fear only makes her pussy feel hotter as it gushes with a painful excitement. She had not imagined the taste of leather, but it doesn't surprise her she can't resist it even though it possesses no real flavor. His thumb slips between her lips and she instantly craves to experience more of him even as she dreads this need, terrified of where it will lead. His other hand grips her hip, and she moans again in a hopeless confusion of shame and longing as his hard-on digs into the cheeks of her ass through his leather pants.

"Would you like him to fuck you, Miranda?" Richard asks kindly.

Alex empties her mouth of his thumb so she can respond .

"No!" she whispers. "Please!"

"Please *what*, Miranda? His voice suddenly sounds uncannily like Michael's. "There's nothing to be ashamed of, sweetheart, be honest with yourself. Your pussy's soaking wet, isn't it? I don't even need to feel it to know it is, and it's not something you can lie about. No amount of mental guilt can hide the physical evidence of how you truly feel and of what you really want."

"Oh, God, you promised you were only going to sketch me!"

"If that was all you wanted me to do, but that's not all you really want to happen, is it, Miranda?"

"I think the mistake is letting her believe she has a choice," Alex points out firmly.

"That's true," Richard agrees, his voice drawing closer.

Alex tightens his grip on her neck and thrusts his other hand between her legs, forcing them apart as far as her bound ankles allow. "Mm, yes..." He slips two fingers into her slick sex. "She's so sweet, so tight, and wet like you wouldn't believe."

His gloved fingers penetrating her make her pussy weep with a bottomless need that causes her subconscious to begin losing hold of the dream even as she tries desperately to cling to it...

She rolls over in bed, clutching a pillow against her chest in an agony of disappointment. It was only a dream! Richard hadn't touched her except to untie her after he finished sketching her, thanking her for being such a wonderfully cooperative model. But he asked her to pose for him again, offering to pay her directly so she wouldn't have to give the college a commission, and the look in his eyes told her if she agreed to come back on her own, and allowed him to tie her up a second time, that the results of the sitting would be much more memorable than a few mediocre sketches. She accepted his phone number and promised him she'd think about it even though she fully intended not to think about it because she had a boyfriend she was madly in love with, yet her dream has made it frighteningly obvious love has nothing to do with it, just like the lyrics of that song she hates. She is irresistibly drawn to a man like Richard, a man who can take her in hand and give her everything she doesn't even know she wants, everything she needs, whatever it turns out to be. Her pussy is wet from her dream, yet would she really enjoy being fucked by a faceless stranger simply because he was wearing black leather and knew just how to talk to her, just how to handle her? It's a very scary thought indeed, yet in the last few weeks she has learned enough about herself to actually consider the possibility.

She flings the pillow away and reaches for the phone. She has to talk to someone about this, and there's only Sarah to call even though she's sure Michael would understand. She can ask him to wear black leather pants and coats and gloves to excite her. But would it be the same? She craves the dark magic of other men, handsome strangers with an absolute thrilling power over her thoughts and feelings. She has found her soul mate at last, and here she is in danger of allowing a growing obsession with sexual fantasies to destroy her very real happiness. It's inconceivable. She has to get help.

Richard's card is lying by the phone, as if she doesn't need to keep it a secret, but really because she isn't seeing Michael until the weekend so she has plenty of time to conceal it.

She fully intends to call Sarah, but it is another number she dials, and a man's voice that answers.

Chapter Sixteen

Michael raised his head and looked around him. There was no one else in the small room hung with paintings deep in the labyrinth of the M.F.A. The security guard had wandered off into another gallery, hands clasped behind his back, walking as slowly as he could to make the progress from one room to another last as long as possible. Michael never ceased to wonder how they could stand such a mind-numbingly boring job, yet they always greeted him cheerfully and looked happy enough. He tried to see it from their perspective – they were indoors where it was warm, and even though they were obliged to stand all day they weren't doing hard physical labor for their monthly paychecks. Some of them probably also liked the authority the uniform gave them, minimal as it was. More often than not, the highlight of their day was gently pulling a five-year-old and her sticky fingers away from a priceless masterpiece. He didn't believe security guards all secretly wanted to be cops. Their gentle beat was across polished wooden floors and whisper-quiet carpets, and the people they protected, all imprisoned in ornate frames, threatened only their self-esteem as they wondered why they weren't as impressed by them as society told them they should be.

Michael new the names of most of the security guards in the Museum of Fine Arts. Grateful for someone to talk to, they let him get as close to a painting as he wanted to, and more than one of them had allowed him to caress the sleek buttocks of a marble statue, looking away discreetly while sipping the coffee from *Starbuck's* he brought them. They allowed him to set his easel up wherever he desired, and they knew when to wander away into another room and leave him alone. Once he began unpacking his supplies he didn't feel like talking anymore, his eyes fixed on the masterpiece he was intent on exploring that day. There was nothing like sketching the figures in a painting to get a feel for their flow, seemingly so effortless, but really such a technically difficult task that he had become a firm believer in talent as a force guiding the artist's hand mysteriously independent of the brain, which it merely possessed and used for its own ends.

"Man, you're good." His favorite guard, an old black man named Reggie, exclaimed over his shoulder one afternoon without lowering his voice to the church-like hush everyone adopted in museums for some reason. Michael loved spending whole afternoons in the M.F.A. because it was a hell of a lot warmer than his apartment. He couldn't afford to fill his heating tank until the beginning of the month because he was short on cash – he had happily spent more than he should have on Miranda – and he had disciplined himself not to dip into his Trust Fund unless he encountered a life-threatening emergency. Nevertheless, cozy as the well-heated rooms were, part of him hated the morgue-like atmosphere of museums. Works of art were sensual, living things in his eyes that belonged in homes where they could add magic to everyday life; where they could deepen a person's appreciation for the beauty of the world and the human body. But of course, only the wealthiest souls could afford their own private works, everyone else had to settle for reproductions that couldn't possibly capture the subtle depth and luminosity of the originals.

It was Friday afternoon and he was having a hard time concentrating on art. He was thinking about Miranda. He was always thinking about Miranda even when he was busy doing other things; the scent and feel, the exquisite intensity of her, never left him. But today, especially, he couldn't get her out of his head. He was haunted by the way her voice had sounded yesterday morning when she called him, apologizing for waking him up, but she had to talk to him. And the things she said were imbuing the day, and everything surrounding him, with a dream-like sharpness, making him even more acutely aware of how sensual, even darkly erotic, most of the paintings surrounding him were. He had set up in front of a nymph clad in a diaphanous Greek *chiton*. She perched nearly suspended above the ground, her waist embraced by a dark young god's strong arm as he stole her away, a powerful wind pressing the transparent material against her tender belly and breasts, her pink nipples erect beneath her parted lips and half frightened eyes looking behind her at the normal world she was forsaking for a desire she was not sure she could trust… for a lust whose divine nature would either keep her magically safe or destroy her…

He flipped the page on his drawing pad, glancing over his shoulder, glad the room was empty. He wasn't sketching the painting before him. His hand had wandered with his mind. A stark rendering of Miranda on her knees and bent over some amorphous surface, her hands tied behind her back, had taken form in stark black, white and red as he deliberately marked her slender body with hot red whip marks, cruelly striping her back and the tender space of her thighs.

He wondered what Reggie would make of this piece of work, and smiled to himself. He couldn't believe she was his, but she definitely was and (he had almost immediately accepted this rather daunting responsibility) she always would be. He was glad he knew he loved her before she asked him to spank her, and especially before everything she confessed to him on the phone yesterday morning. That conversation was forever branded into his brain, and it was still smoldering in his groin. He thought of his father, the handsome cop in the black uniform that fit him so well, and the black leather gloves he wore in winter, handcuffs dangling from his lean hips at once threatening and promising to girls like Miranda. It was ironic he had decided not to follow in his dad's footsteps and thereby given up the uniform that would have turned his girlfriend on so much. Yet it seemed that, after all, he was destined to wear black leather gloves and to snap handcuffs on bad girls, *his* beautiful and *very* bad girl with the heart of a gold. Her sharp, profoundly poetic mind filled him with wonder and faith in himself because she saw so much good in him; because she trusted him and loved him without any reservations.

It was no use trying to concentrate on painted bodies today. He couldn't get Miranda's flesh-and-blood figure out of his mind and all the things she had confessed she wanted him to do to her. He began packing up his supplies going over in his head again some of the things she had said – some of the scenarios she had dared paint for him. At first she was evasively coy, shyly hinting at things. Torn between excitement and impatience, he had commanded her to tell him everything, and to go into as much detail as possible because it was the only way he could understand her and give her what she wanted. He didn't say he would *try* to fulfill her darkest erotic desires; he knew he could and he would; he even wanted to. His only concern was that the reality would be too much for her; that she only believed she desired these things. He hoped not, because it was too late for her to change her mind now; he wasn't going to let her off that easy. She had awakened appetites in him that had lain dormant within him ready to his emerge. He had been born with creative abilities, they were in his blood, and God – or whatever – had kindly sent him a sexually submissive and profoundly kinky model who could exercise both his talents as a sensitive artist and as a dominant male. It seemed too good to be true – so many men would figuratively or even literally kill to be in his shoes – but it also wasn't going to be easy developing his technical skills as a painter while handling an intensely gorgeous creature like Miranda. He knew the minute he snapped handcuffs on her that a part of her would question everything she had told him, everything she had confessed about herself, because they were, after all, still only fantasies safely contained in her mind. Fleshing them out in reality so their relationship didn't suffer was going to be as hard as painting a masterpiece, but he was more than willing to try. It turned him on knowing she would spend a good part of her day sitting at the computer writing a detailed description of a possible kinky scenario. During that fateful phone call, he had said to her, "Tell me everything it is you think you want, Miranda. Don't hold back. This won't be easy for either one of us, so you have to be absolutely honest with yourself and with me if we're going to make this work. I have some fantasies, you know how much I enjoyed spanking you, but I need to know how far I can really go; how far you want me to go. But be careful, because what you write, I'll make you live. For both our sakes, I have no intention of disappointing you." He then commanded her to e-mail him the document before seven o'clock that evening. He intended to savor it along with pizza and beer while making his plans for tomorrow.

* * *

Miranda's e-mail:

Dear Michael,

I don't really know where to start, and I don't even know if I really want to analyze what I've discovered about my desires all that much, I just know that they're there, that they're intense, and that they turn me on almost beyond my ability to control, and even though that's frightening, it's also so exciting...

Sarah said to me once that I could get away with murder because I'm so beautiful, and I think she's right in a way, and this may have something to do with my desire to be disciplined. I think maybe it's a key to understanding my need for a truly dominant man who isn't afraid, or lovingly hesitant, to give me what I need, a man who craves doing these things to me for his own reasons, so that my excitement is never dimmed by wondering if he's just doing it to please me. All my life I've gotten away with so much, even fooling myself by writing about something so beautifully it felt true, at least for a while, even though deep down I knew it wasn't and that I was just surrendering to a shamefully overriding desire to reach a comfortable conclusion. I think that's one of my major character flaws, that I value feeling comfortable and safe even while craving intense experiences as well, but without all the emotional strain and mess that often accompanies them. Does that make any sense? But, for better or for worse, my soul won't let me get away with it. I realize now how much my soul *needs* intensity, and maybe that's one reason I crave punishment, because the deepest part of me is chas-

—

tising other more superficial aspects of my personality it knows need to be made less dominant than they are for my own spiritual good. And pain is not comfortable, pain is a neurological "mess", and it's also the quickest way to experience pure intensity. In pain my soul is hauntingly at peace because every single part of me glimpses, and is forced to accept, the reality of an energy, of a force, that transcends thought and even time and space and reason in its throes. The pain when you spanked me put every part of me in touch, for a few terribly transcendent moments, with the very real possibility that my abstract philosophical belief in an eternal spirit that forges and burns out the vehicles of its bodies might actually be true. And afterwards, I'm primordially hot and wet and ready to be shaped like all the sensuality of matter mysteriously born in the burning core of a star...

I'm not glossing things over here, Michael, and using metaphysical imagery to get away from how I really feel, it *is* how I really feel. There's a "pagan" quality to the act of submitting to, and being mysteriously disciplined, by a strong and deeply confident man like you that evokes echoes of priestesses and high priests in my psyche. It isn't about humiliation – it's about transcendence. And of course it's also about fear, because we can't ever really know what happens to our feelings beyond our flesh. I'm starting to think that, for me, the idea of kinky sex is about daring to walk this haunting bridge – about daring to identify with the mysterious energy inside ourselves that uses our body, that shapes and commands it, and hates being subject to the petty fears of the mortal ego, which so often gets the better of us in this time and place in history, and that needs desperately to be put in its place. I think that, these days, there's a need for some violence in sex because we've lost touch with the earth as part of ourselves and our own sensuality. We're abusing the planet, and killing so many parts of her in species that have vanished forever, that I think the pain of punishment is a therapeutic way to empathize with the pain my soul feels night and day because of this.

Do you understand that I'm not just being evasively "over the top" when I say these things, Michael? It's really becoming clear to me how much my beliefs form a vital part of my libido. I've learned lately that the darker and more intense sex is, the more it turns me on in the moment and feels spiritual to me afterwards. Pleasure is a wonderful part of the sensual world, but it's not about walking on the edge, not about slipping on black leather like priestly vestments...

But you told me to write you a detailed description of some of the things I imagine you doing to me, so here goes...

I want you to be really hard on me, Michael, because I can really be a very, very bad girl. I want you to spank me with your naked hand like you did on Christmas Eve, but this time with my body bent over your hard knees while you're still fully dressed, all in black. You strip off my shirt first, but you don't bother to remove my short skirt; you just bunch it up around my waist while the tips of my naked breasts graze against your black pants. It's not a comfortable position at all, yet I love how hard your legs are against me. "Please don't give me more than fifty strokes, Michael, please!" I beg. I've never been spanked really hard for so long, and I know I won't be able to stand it, not at all. Your response is to bring your hand down hard on my ass in a loud slap that stings and burns so much it's inconceivable I can stand much more. "You're getting one-hundred stokes just like I promised you, Miranda. This is what you wanted. Don't forget that." I moan because of course it's true, but I don't understand it at all now. Yet it's not about what my mind wants at all – it's about what my soul desperately needs in this world. I go as limp as I can across your lap, one hand clutching the bedspread, the other one your pants leg, making an effort to brace myself, and I'm so grateful when you firmly grip the back of my neck with one hand that

I whimper. My hair is flowing forward, hiding my face; it's easy for you to get a grip on my neck and fully exercise the power your strong grip has over me. All I can see is the floor and the edge of my innocent white shirt, and there *is* something truly innocent about my belief in the soul and its needs, a mysterious virtue that paradoxically demands a dark and violent act from the man across whose knees I'm draped like a flesh-and-blood doll craving the animating force of his punishment like life itself…

You begin spanking me hard, Michael, and after the first five or so blows I know I can't take any more. I'm more and more grateful for the way you're clutching my neck, holding me down, almost threatening to cut off my breath if I keep squirming and making a vain effort to writhe out of reach of your unbelievably hard hand. By the tenth stroke it's impossible for me to believe there's ninety more to come, it's as impossible as believing I can survive the death of my body as I feel more excruciatingly, agonizingly trapped in my flesh than ever before. Yet believing anything is irrelevant because I really can't think at all except to be amazed by the radiating, all-consuming power of the pain. I didn't expect the sting in the burn, the blindingly sharp searing sensation that's like being cut and burned at the same time. My tender ass is on fire, all the outraged blood cells rushing to the surface of my sensitive skin burning hot as suns melting the core of my flesh and making my pussy inconceivably hot and wet. I'm aware of my sex helplessly juicing even through the agony as it reaches a climax beyond which it can't get any worse, and yet it doesn't ebb, not at all. It's like a workout, the first few minutes are the hardest before the endorphins get flowing and begin transforming the ordeal into something else… every time your hand comes down the pain still blows my mind, but I like that, I'm mysteriously free of all guilt and responsibility, of all thought, and I stop pretending to struggle to get away. You're being as hard on me as you said you would be, and I'm so glad

157

about this that I'm crying with relief and gratitude. This spanking is the worst and the best thing that has ever happened to me. There's no chance of being disappointed by the intensity of the experience because it's absolutely killing me, and I love that, I hate it and I love it, I hate it and I love it… your hand beating down on me, my heart beating faster and faster as if perversely trying to get away from how undeniably alive you're making me feel…

When it's finally over, your hand has forged your willpower directly into me – I'm completely limp and willing for you to do whatever you desire with me. I'm glad when you help me up, because your hard knees are making it hard for me to breathe, and when you push me gently face down across the bed, I relax gratefully across it for a moment with my eyes closed. I feel my exposed pussy silently begging for you to fuck me, the flesh of my ass cheeks screaming the same tormented need for the deep, soothing relief of your hard dick plunging in and out of me. But I don't know if you'll fuck me, I don't know what you'll do next…

It doesn't matter. The important thing is I really know I can trust you now to be truly hard on me, as hard as I want you to be. The spanking you just gave me was so fulfilling, yet it also feels like just the beginning of truly being able to live other even darker pleasures with you…

I feel you bending over me as you caress my burning bottom, not really soothing the ache; I don't feel it's as much concern as appreciation prompting your touch, which turns me on almost more than I can bear…

I roll over onto my back, turn my body around, and hang my head off the edge of the bed. "Let me suck you, please!" I beg, reaching back for your thighs, mindlessly hungry, desperate to feel your erection filling my mouth. I moan with gratitude when you open your pants and give me what I need without taking your clothes off. You just pull your dick out and slip it between my lips, and I'm blissfully confident you won't hesitate now to fuck my throat as hard as you spanked me. In this position you can get your entire hard-on into my mouth and neck, and part of me is appalled that I've willingly gone from one intense discomfort to another and that I'm loving it. You taste so good to me, you always do, and the bigger and harder you get, the more difficult it is for me to breathe, but I want more than anything for you to be able to use me this way. I spread my legs open and clutch the bedspread, aching to feel another hard cock driving into my pussy. I want it so much I'm almost literally able to feel it plunging in and out of me, as if your vicious spanking activated dark forces swirling around my soaking wet sex lips so the very air seems to be sensually licking me. I groan when you reach down and clutch my breasts, bracing yourself on them as you ram your erection deep into my throat. You climax with your scrotum pressed with suffocating selfishness against my face, and I nearly gag as your cum spurts down my neck, but I resist the urge and relish the sensation, very happy I pleased you, fervently hoping I did...

Did I please you, Michael?

Love,

Miranda

Chapter Seventeen

Three Months Later

Spring was more astonishingly beautiful than ever that year in Boston. Someone had placated the rain gods and they stayed away, letting the sun shine and the flowers bloom and the sky glow a deeply radiant blue impossible to describe even as it pulled all your senses outside so your eyes could gaze up in awe. It was the best time of year to picnic in a graveyard.

Miranda and Michael caught a bus in Harvard Square that dropped them off almost directly in front of the black wrought-iron gates of Mount Auburn Cemetery. He was traveling light today, sandwiches and bottled water filling his backpack instead of art supplies, a credit-card sized digital camera slipped into a pocket of his black jeans. Miranda was entirely free of any burdens except a delicious unease as she wondered what he had planned for her. She had dressed to his specifications – a loose black skirt just long enough for her to get away with not wearing any panties beneath it, knee-high black boots with white socks, a formfitting black sweater that buttoned all the way down in front, and no bra. She knew from experience this attire provided him with easy access to all her most intimate parts, and she was glad the weather had warmed up enough that going without undergarments was a pleasure rather than a problem. Yet there was still a decided chill in the air even on an April day so glorious it almost stunned her senses; the clarity of shapes and the intensity of colors beating against the nerve ends in her eyes as a sudden cold breeze reminded her winter could still return in full force as it slipped up her skirt, and found all the tiny spaces between the buttons on her shirt. Her nipples carving themselves against the clinging black cashmere had attracted some attention in Harvard Square. It seemed to please Michael when other men stared at her; he was too confident of her feelings for him to be jealous, and this absolute lack of insecurity in him bound her to him more profoundly with each passing day and night. The unyieldingly firm, yet also tenderly loving control he had taken of her since that night months ago when she first asked him to spank her was the way she had always dreamed of a man treating her. She had her safe word, but she never used it. It surprised her that the darkly erotic world they entered together had well defined paths marked with very reasonable and clear-cut rules. She understood the term *subculture* better than she ever had in school now that she was part of one. She had a B.A. in World Lit, but lately she felt cheated. Surely there were clues hidden in the works of writers throughout the ages expounding on the dark desires inside her she had only stumbled upon by chance. Miranda was no stranger to Mount Auburn Cemetery; she and Sarah had come here more than once to discuss everything from the virtues and limitations of the world's religions, to all the problems and dis-appointments they were inevitably encountering with their latest boyfriends. She felt guilty about hardly spending time with Sarah in the last few months but, strangely enough, it was easier to talk about frustrations and unrealized longings than it was to express how happy and fulfilled she was. Unhappiness was hard, it cast long, well defined shadow-sentences, whereas happiness was like a bright light suffusing every cell of her mind and body in a way that was difficult to put into words. Describing the things she and Michael did together could not possibly convey the stimulating and nurturing effect their relationship had on her. She had written more than one poem but she still wasn't happy with any of them – something about her feelings being his private garden as he penetrated her flesh and her psyche, violently and relentlessly sowing the seeds of his desires inside her until they became an indelible part of her; her sensuality blooming around him as never before because he always dug deep enough to arouse her soul as well as her body. Her metaphysical bent was so much a part of her sex drive, it explained why she had never truly been satisfied before Patrick literally shoved her off the straight and narrow path when he pushed her back against the door and opened up a whole new world.

They walked side-by-side in silence, matching strides, and she was proud of herself for keeping up with him so effortlessly. They headed away from the entrance as quickly as possible, the profound silence of the cemetery enfolding them as they left the road far behind.

She never ceased to be morbidly amazed by the monstrosities some peo-ple commissioned for their supposed eternal resting places, including a hideous stone sphinx and a small pyramid that made her cringe with their Victorian stiffness; they possessed none of the sensual power and grace of the ancient Egyptian originals. Bad taste was creepy enough when you were alive, but to be stuck with it for all eternity was truly disturbing. Of course, none of the people who had dreamed up these pathetically grandiose monuments were still actually there... and yet there was something invigorating about the air in the cemetery that had nothing to do with the beautiful Spring day; she could not be entirely sure she was completely alone with her lover. It seemed almost likely that some of the residents had grown obsessively fond of the particular body they had buried here. She felt that way about some old dresses hanging in the back of her closet she would never wear again for one reason or another yet still couldn't bring herself to throw out because they reminded her of moments she experienced while wearing them. Maybe cemeteries were scrapbooks of the spirit, the gravestones and the coffins beneath them filled with memories invisible to the naked eye but not to the mysterious energy of souls sentimentally clinging to their past...

"Oh weird..."

Michael glanced at her without breaking his stride. "What?"

"Nothing... I just always have the wildest thoughts when I come here."

"Mm."

She glanced at him, a tingle of anxiety rushing up her spine as the breeze found the edge of her shirt and slipped chillingly inside it again. His face looked unusually hard today, or maybe it was only her nervous imagination trying to figure out what kinky scene he had planned for them that made it appear that way to her, but she didn't think so; she had become very sensitive to all the subtleties of his expressions. His mouth could embody infinite degrees of tenderness and firmness she had learned to read like a thermometer revealing the depth of his pleasure or displeasure with her. His eyes were also marvelously communicative. Sometimes when he looked at her they shone with such a vulnerable depth of love, she glimpsed the breathtaking truth of her power over him no matter how many commands he gave her and how roughly he used her.

He veered off the path and she followed him, climbing a few feet behind him up a hill, then down, and then up a steep ravine, until she felt wonderfully lost in the rolling landscape of magnificent old trees just coming into leaf above eternal stone homes of every imaginable shape and size. She glimpsed the delightfully sinister-looking entrance to a mausoleum between the branches of a weeping willow, and soon it was obvious Michael was heading right for it.

For two reasons, she had learned to put a big red virtual STOP sign in front of all speculative thoughts whenever he made it clear he was going to make demands on her – because her imagination was never quite equal to his, and because the debilitating flashes of fear she experienced not knowing what was to come perversely stoked her excitement. She usually had no idea what was in store for her, and she both resented this fact and loved it. Her feelings were a profound gray zone in the straightforwardly sunny day – a darkly charged sexual current in haunting harmony with the hard tombstones weathered by decades of wind and rain, sun and sleet relentlessly caressing them. Her mingled fear and arousal felt deeper than the graves around them. She knew she could trust Michael to push her almost beyond her limits, and there was something intensely spiritual about this… death as a darkly violent lover pushing us beyond our limits, beyond pain and fear, forcing us to realize how much more we really are…

The mausoleum was locked, of course, which was slightly disappointing but also, she had to admit, a big relief. She didn't share her mixed feelings with Michael as she followed him silently around the building, pretending not to really care one way or the other if he found a way in, which he seemed determined to do. The small mortuary temple was located in a very secluded spot, flanked on all sides by steep hills, its weathered stone nearly invisible surrounded by three ancient weeping willows, their naked branches still a lifeless grey. At least the place was private enough, but she suspected her lover's unorthodox desires were, for once, going to be frustrated because there was no way into the building that she could see except the locked door. She should have known it was always a mistake to underestimate him, and her tendency to continue doing so despite all the times he had proven her wrong vaguely shamed her, deepening her conviction that she deserved his discipline. She watched, chastened, as he shrugged his backpack off in front of a single small window in one of the walls. There was no glass in the frame, just four black wrought iron bars. She could hardly believe it, and yet she was not truly surprised, when he produced a tool he had brought along in a separate compartment of the pack in order not to crush the hummus and broccoli sprout sandwiches she had made for them.

"What are you doing, Michael?" she asked despite herself. She knew perfectly well what he was doing, and he knew she knew. He would not bother responding to a question that almost literally squeaked out of her as she shamefully sided with a frightened, mousy side of her personality instead of with the wildly sensual pussy they both new perfectly well she was deep down whenever she dared to be.

She watched in growing admiration and trepidation as he wrenched the iron bars out of their sockets one after the other, dropping them onto the ground at his feet. He was wearing black leather boots, tight black jeans, and a form-fitting black sweater with a scoop neck that set off his broad shoulders and teased her with a glimpse of his hard chest. His jeans were held up by a black leather belt she had felt against her naked flesh more than once, and she savored the memory now like the sweet bitterness of very dark chocolate. Once she even had to cancel her scheduled sittings for two days because of the marks his belt left on her ass and the backs of her thighs. They learned to be more careful after that, although it thrilled her when he threatened to one day make her take the stand with all the evidence of what a bad girl she was visible to an entire room of people.

"You don't expect me to climb up in there do you?" she heard herself ask incredulously. She couldn't stop herself even though she hated how pathetic she sounded.

"I do, and you will," he replied shortly, lifting his pack and tossing it casually into the tomb. It landed with a dull thud echoed by her heart speeding up.

"But I can't reach it, Michael…" She kept trying to save herself from the inevitable, wondering why she even bothered. She really *did* deserve to be spanked for being such a silly coward; for being afraid of scraping her knees on the rough stone; for being so lazy she would let a few seconds of discomfort ruin all the possible fun they could have in there.

"Come here," he commanded, sinking to one knee and lacing the fingers of his hands together.

She obeyed him, but now she was afraid of hurting him as she tentatively rested her right foot in the cradle he provided for her. The excruciatingly hard palms that had spanked her more times than she could count seemed tender and vulnerable now beneath her square heel.

"Ready?" he demanded.

"Yes!" She reached for the windowsill as he straightened up and lifted her with him. She heaved herself onto the ledge, and he helped her drape her right leg over it.

"That's my girl."

The approval in his voice gave her the strength to pull her left leg up until she was kneeling on the ledge like a cat. Her loose pleated skirt had not inhibited her movements, and she understood why he had wanted her to wear it. There was also no denying the fact that it pleased her how acutely conscious she became of her smoothly shaved pussy when the tender crown of her mons rubbed against the rough stone, giving her clit a macabre kiss that instantly had her warm juices responding to the chilly lick of the breeze. She carefully turned and sat down, hanging her legs over the other side of the sill facing into the crypt.

"Michael, it's really dark in here!"

"Can you see the floor?"

"No!"

"Let your eyes adjust for a minute."

"Okay…"

"Can you see it now?"

"Yes…"

"Good."

"But…"

"Jump, Miranda. I'll be right in."

Over three months of responding to that particular tone in his voice told her there was no hope of turning back. She plunged into the tomb. The floor wasn't as far below her as it had looked, but it was made of stone, and the sound of her heels coming into contact with it echoed loudly, accusingly around her. She barely missed crushing the lovingly prepared sandwiches in his backpack. She grabbed it, pulling it out of the way as his silhouette carved itself from the square of light above her.

He landed more quietly than she did.

"What are we doing in here, Michael?" She had to ask.

He squatted by the pack and quickly produced two white pillar candles, handing one up to her along with a lighter.

She flicked it gratefully to life, moving out of the faint shaft of light from the window. The warmly luminous halo born in the darkness as the wick caught was only a sad ghost of the sun rising over a ponderous black marble altar. In its center sat a white urn-like vase filled with real flowers, not the long-lasting plastic blooms she might have expected, their delicate beauty a tragic echo of life's fragility in the shadowy stillness.

"Someone was here recently," she observed anxiously.

"Then they probably won't be coming back anytime soon," Michael pointed out reasonably, setting his burning candle on one end of the altar and revealing a row of metal plaques behind it inscribed with the names of the six people forever filed away in the wall.

She was relieved to know there were no bones in the mausoleum, only ashes. "Isn't this just a little... disrespectful?" she said uncertainly. "I mean, these are people's loved ones in there..."

He took the candle and the lighter out of her hand, slipping the latter into his pocket, and placing the former on the other end of the marble slab. "Does being in here make you feel sinfully wicked, Miranda?"

"No, just *disrespectful*," she snapped.

He came and stood before her, tilting her face up to his as if admiring the way the flickering light licked her features out of the darkness. "But there's no one here except us," he said quietly.

"We can't be entirely sure of that," she whispered stubbornly.

"That's true, we can't," he whispered back, beginning to unbutton her shirt from the bottom up, making it clear he intended for her to take it off completely, not just expose her breasts.

"Michael, it's cold in here," she protested.

"Is it really, Miranda? I don't think you're just afraid of catching cold."

"No..." She hated him for being so mercilessly astute all the time, for not letting her get away with anything, and she worshipped him for it.

"Then what *are* you afraid of?" Before she could respond, he turned her around and slipped the shirt down her arms.

"I'm afraid someone will come in and see us and we'll be arrested!" she blurted.

"I thought you liked being handcuffed." He turned her back to face him, and her indignation melted away when she saw the teasing smile on his face. "It'll be fine," he assured her lightly. "No one's coming except you." He unzipped her skirt and let it slip down her legs.

She stepped out of the pleated folds, savoring his promising threat as he led her over to the altar, and then lifted her onto its edge. It made her intensely nervous being so far away from her clothes, dropped carelessly onto a floor that might not have been swept in decades, although the vase of fresh flowers enabled her to hope it had been more recently cleaned. Then how sensually smooth her nude skin appeared caressed by candlelight from both ends distracted her with the sexy vulnerability of her slender body resting against the unyielding stone as she lay back. She was too high up for him to simply open his pants and fuck her, and she discovered that wasn't what he intended at all as he pushed open her thighs, bent over, and lightly kissed her clit.

She moaned in expectant surprise. This was the last thing she had pictured happening inside the crypt – her commanding lover going down on her. Suddenly, she liked that the edge of the marble dug into the tender cheeks of her bottom as he slipped his arms beneath her legs and pulled her body over the edge into his face. She gasped as he captured her mysteriously sensitive seed between his lips, and sucked on it gently for a minute before licking her slit, running his firm tongue from the very bottom of her labia all the way back up over and over again with escalating ferocity...

She was off, transported on the dark waves of fantasies lapping with increasing vividness through her mind on the cresting pleasure, which was deep and dark and luminous all at the same time, its faint glow flickering in her nerve-ends gradually blooming to a glorious warmth in her pelvis. Her fear of them being caught dissolved as she ascended beyond all such irrelevant concerns on the angelic wings of an unfolding orgasm even as he growled like a demon and yanked her sex even harder against him. He was fucking her with his lips and his tongue, with is teeth and his nose, all his handsome features carving themselves into her soft wet folds. She cried out and reached for the edges of the marble slab to brace herself, his tongue penetrating her, then orbiting her clit, stoking her orgasm with such unbearable slowness she struggled to push herself over the edge by writhing against his face. She was desperate to feel all her most special muscles contracting, and squeezing a transcendent joy through her blood as she ascended above everything lying naked deep in a crypt...

Her cries rebounded against the stone walls as she came with mind blowing intensity, and then she couldn't seem to stop coming as he wedged three fingers into her spasming cunt, painfully prolonging the ecstasy.

"Now if *that* doesn't wake the dead," he said, "nothing will."

She laughed breathlessly, the marrow in her bones feeling momentarily pulverized; reduced to ashes by the impact of her climax. Her soaking pussy left a warm, perfumed offering on the cold black stone.

"Don't *you* want to come?" she asked weakly.

He grasped her hands and helped her sit up. "Not here. Get dressed. The day has only just begun."

"Yes, Michael," she said, as ever stabbed deep in her sex by a double-edged excitement and dread.

Chapter Eighteen

Miranda was passing the time before Michael's arrival looking at some of the X-rated pictures he had taken of her with his digital camera. He e-mailed them to her, and she filed them away by time and place. This evening she was studying some of the images he shot of her at Mount Auburn Cemetery. He hadn't been kidding – her long hard day *had* only just begun after he treated her to an orgasm in a mausoleum. The climax of her ordeals had come at the top of a tower with a panoramic view of the beautiful graveyard. She couldn't see anything, however, except the inside of the empty room. He made her strip off all her clothes again, letting her keep her black leather boots on, then instructed her to sit with her back against the wall directly beneath one of the narrow castle-like windows. He raised her arms over her head and handcuffed her wrists to one of the black wrought-iron bars. It was not an uncomfortable position, until he told her to rest her legs straight against the floor and spread them open as far she could. Physically, she could have held that pose quite some time, it was his eyes openly assessing her totally exposed sex that made her squirm. The lips of her labia were pulled apart, making her embarrassingly conscious of the insatiable hole at the heart of her vulva. She knew from having studied her sex in a mirror what the entrance into her body looked like – a wetly gleaming darkness at its heart, her salty cream shimmering around it on her labia's slick and rosy folds evoking sea shells haunted by the echo of life as she longed to be filled by a cock. But of course, all analogies failed when it came to describing the lush wonder of her pussy, as Michael pointed out to her that afternoon while taking pictures of her inviting openness and her contrastingly reserved expression above it. She couldn't believe the way he talked to her that day in the cemetery; it turned her on even more than being tied up and helpless in a stone tower. It made the cold seeping into her nude body irrelevant... no, it made the chilly discomfort of her flesh an exciting sacrifice as she offered herself up on the altar of his penetrating appreciation, and was rewarded by an even deeper respect for herself and her desirable beauty.

The computer clock told her he was ten minutes late, which wasn't like him; he was almost uncannily punctual, as if the train and bus schedules obeyed the silent command of his willpower to arrive the minute he ran onto the platform. She shut off her monitor and walked restlessly into the living room. Her red curtains were open to the sky even though winter was making one last stand; clouds that threatened yet another snowfall dimmed the luminous enchantment of twilight, her favorite hour. The vegetable lasagna she had prepared earlier was waiting to be slipped into the oven, and she had glasses of wine ready on the counter to be filled by either red or white, whatever he desired tonight. She perched on the edge of the loveseat, wondering if she should turn on the TV while she waited, but the anxiety suddenly possessing her would make it impossible to concentrate on anything. Something was wrong, she could feel it.

She stood up restlessly, and almost at once heard the key she had given him months ago turn in the lock. She smiled with relief, walking quickly towards the door, ready to greet him with a passionate hug and kiss. His expression when he entered stopped her short. He stood on the threshold looking at her almost as if he had never seen her before; as if he had walked into the wrong apartment.

"What's wrong?" she gasped.

Slowly, deliberately, he closed the door behind him. "Look outside," he said quietly.

Without letting herself think, she turned and hurried over to the window. When she saw the heating oil truck parked at the curb, she closed her eyes, terrifyingly unable to see the rest of her life; her future had suddenly gone as black as the inside of her eyelids. But she had no choice, she had to face him. Their eyes met across the living room and she realized that, somehow, he knew everything now.

"Your *friend* is in the building." He spoke in an undertone seemingly devoid of feelings as he made an obvious effort to keep them under control. "And it just so happens I know him."

"You *know* him?" she repeated blankly, abruptly caught in a nightmare from which she might never awaken.

"Yeah, I grew up a few blocks from his house. He's a friend of the family."

"*Patrick?*" she whispered in sickening disbelief, and then shock began rendering her blessedly numb. She was so stunned she couldn't seem to feel anything except an overwhelming desire to travel back in time and undo what she had done, but it was impossible, and if she did she wouldn't be standing where she was now, helplessly in love with the man looking at her in a way that made her want to die.

"Yes, *Patrick*. My mom and his wife have been friends ever since I can remember."

"I *told* you about him, Michael…"

"Yes, you did." His voice was cold, but at least he walked towards her. "I was surprised to see him, I didn't realize he made deliveries all the way in Arlington. He was on his way up here." He stopped a hand's breath away from her, looking down into her eyes as if searching for something vital he had lost and there was nowhere else for him to look. "We were both on our way up here, imagine that. I don't know which one of us was more surprised."

"He delivers oil to everyone in this building…" she argued weakly.

"He said, 'Michael! What are you doing here'? 'Hey, Pat', I said, not putting two and two together right away because I was actually happy to see him again, 'my girlfriend lives here'. 'In apartment nine'? he asks. 'Yeah, how'd you know'? But he didn't answer, instead he looked at me real hard and muttered, 'So you're the one she's so madly in love with'. I couldn't have been more surprised if he'd punched me in the gut. 'How do you know about us'? I blurted like an idiot, before I finally remembered the little fling you had with a married man before we met. 'When was the last time you saw, her'? I asked, and you know what he told me, Miranda? He looked me straight in the eye, and realizing I knew he'd fucked you, and that it was no good trying to pretend he hadn't, he told me the last time he saw you was the day before Christmas."

Even though she knew he could see the truth in her eyes – the lie she told him even as she confessed to the affair – she was much too in love with him to look away. She knows it wouldn't do any good to tell him she's sorry. She *is* sorry she didn't have the courage to confess the whole truth to him, but even now she's not sorry about the intense experience she shared with

Patrick in the basement. Her brief encounters with him opened her up to the unorthodox nature of her desires in a way she can't possibly regret.

He asked very quietly, *"Was* that the last time he saw you, Miranda?"

"Yes, I swear it was!"

"Really?" He grabbed her face with one hand, pressing his thumb and fingers cruelly into her cheeks. "What are you willing to swear by?"

"My soul!" she breathed.

"You lied to me by not telling me the whole truth, Miranda. You *lied* to me."

"I know," she said miserably, his grip making it even harder for her to speak. "I wish more than anything in the universe I'd had the courage to tell you the whole truth, but I didn't…"

"No, you didn't." He let go of her abruptly as if disgusted to be touching her. "You had an affair with one of my dad's best friends. Way to go, baby." He turned away.

"Michael, don't leave me, *please!"*

"Who said anything about leaving? I'm just going to pour myself a glass of wine." He glanced back at her. "When I get back, you're going to be completely nude and standing in a corner facing the wall."

She obeyed him gladly, possessed by a feverish joy. The fact that he was going to punish her meant he was going to forgive her! He wasn't leaving her, he was punishing her! She quickly stripped naked and faced the corner. All she could see was the intensity of her relief.

She heard him walking back towards the living room, his boots making a firm, menacing sound on the hardwood floor of the corridor. He walked much more slowly than her heart was beating.

"Patrick gave me a piece of advice, Miranda," he informed her abruptly.

She knew better than to turn around or speak.

"He said, 'stay away from her, kid, she'll hurt you'."

She closed her eyes but kept her head up, her arms hanging straight at her sides as she wished he would stop punishing her with words, because nothing could feel worse to her than the emotional pain she was causing him.

"Is that why you want me to hurt you all the time, Miranda, because you knew you hurt me? But I suppose nothing's that simple."

She was grateful he didn't really expect a quick answer to such a labyrinthine question. She heard him set his wine glass down and desperately longed for a drink herself, a selfish, petty desire that shamed her much more than her passionate actions with a married man. "I'll never lie to you again, Michael." She dared to say. "I know you have no reason to believe me, but-"

"I have every reason to believe you, Miranda. I love you."

Her joy deepened to the point where she didn't even tense hearing the sinister hiss of his black leather belt coming off.

"I have to punish you for lying to me, Miranda. This isn't discipline, this isn't a sexy game, this is *punishment*, the real thing, and it's going to hurt, it's going to hurt as much as you've hurt me and even more so you'll remember never to lie to me again. Do you understand?"

"Yes, Michael!" she breathed. "Thank you!"

"Let's see if you feel like thanking me after I'm finished with you."

"Nothing can change how I feel about you, Michael, nothing! I love you more than anything!"

"Really? Were you thinking about me while you fucked another man? No, don't say anything. You're going to tell me all about it later. You're going to give me a blow by blow description of what he did to you, and how you felt, and what you were thinking, but not now. Right now I'm going to punish you, and I'm going to leave marks so that for days, every time you look in the mirror, you'll remember that you lied to me. Are you ready?"

"Yes, Michael…"

"And don't even think of using your safe word. This is punishment."

"Yes, Michael…"

"Should I gag you?"

"No, I won't… I won't scream."

"I think you will, but you can tell your landlady we were watching a horror movie. She would never in a million years believe your boyfriend was whipping you with his belt, would she?"

"No…"

"Step back away from the wall and brace yourself against it with both hands, but first I want all the hair off your back. I'm not just going to beat your soft little ass, not tonight. Tonight every part of you is going to suffer the fact that you lied to me."

Oh my God, she thought, but it was a profound awe she was feeling, not fear; she had used up her ability to dread anything except him leaving her. That he was still there was a blessing, and so too was whatever her body had to suffer for the grace of his forgiveness.

He loves me! He really loves me! The conviction lapped through her brain like a mantra chanted by her soul at every lash of his belt. It was impossible to be prepared as he gave her no warning which part of her body he would strike next. The hard hot lick of leather across the middle of her back was awful, but not as terrible as its snaky recoil against her infinitely tender thighs that made the strokes across her ass feel almost relaxing by comparison. He was right, she wanted to scream, she *needed* to scream to try and exhale some of the agony blazing through her as if all her blood cells had caught fire. Her body and its suffering became the absolute heart of the universe in the darkness behind her closed eyelids as she somehow kept silent, sobbing beneath her breath, whimpering but not screaming, not even crying out. She was terribly grateful for the straightforward misery of his belt slicing into her flesh replacing the guilty unhappiness she had endured for months knowing she had lied to him. She was being purged of her sin now, absolved, her emotional slate wiped clean by the mysteriously redeeming, profoundly healing intensity of the pain; her body willingly sacrificing a few moments of comfort for the sake of her soul, aching with love for the man punishing her so relentlessly it left no room for doubt in any fiber of her being that he truly loved her.

Chapter Nineteen

Michael didn't spend the night with her as they had originally planned he would, and this hurt more than his beating. He made it clear his leaving was part of her punishment, but that didn't make the profound loss of his absence any easier to bear. She left the lasagna in the refrigerator desperately hoping he wouldn't make her suffer for very long, that by some miracle they could enjoy a bottle of wine and a nice dinner tomorrow night, forgetting forever the fact that she had ever lied to him like a bad dream. But there was no chance of forgetting, not for a while (not for her whole life) how severely he had punished her for it. Vitamin E cream, two painkillers, and half a bottle of Chardonnay had soothed the burn enough for her to take a quiet, contented pride in the welts his belt had carved all over the back of her body, from between her shoulder blades to just above her knees. He had applied the lotion himself, commanding her to lie facedown on the bed as he sat on the edge, brusquely caressing the healing botanicals into her outraged skin and making her wince even as she whimpered in gratitude. She felt blessed by all the attention he was giving her after the terrible thing she had done to him, but now he was gone. He was smart enough to understand the empty silence of her apartment was the worst part of her punishment. It was the first time he had beaten her without holding her tenderly afterwards or fucking her as violently as she loved him to fuck her. When it was all over, he pulled her into the bedroom and held her firmly by the arms as she looked over her shoulder, dreading what she would see. She gasped, decidedly shocked by the livid red stripes, yet they also filled her with a mysterious pride that she had been able to endure the hot licks of his belt for so long without screaming or begging him to stop.

She was lying on her stomach on the rug in the living room trying to watch television but really controlling a desperately growing urge to call him. She needed to know if he had gone straight home. She was struggling to suppress a nagging fear that he was planning to revenge himself on her by picking up a girl or two at a bar, something he could easily do, she knew. She supposed it was no more than she deserved, but the mere thought filled her with a murderous despair no amount of alcohol or ibuprofen could subdue.

When the phone rang, she literally leapt to her feet and pounced on it.

"Hello, Miranda Covington. Did I interrupt anything? You sound breathless."

"Richard?" she whispered.

"I'm pleased you remember me."

"Of course I remember you!"

"You never called."

"No…"

"And why is that?"

His quiet, insinuating voice was getting the better of her, and she couldn't believe it. This phone call – and her immediate melting reaction to it deep down inside where no leather belt, no matter how violently wielded, would ever be able to reach – was *not* happening, it couldn't be happening because she would never, ever, lie to Michael again...

When she failed to respond, he said firmly, "I would like you to model for me again."

I can't..."

"And why is that?" he repeated quietly.

"Because, I can't do any modeling for a while."

"I'm sorry to hear that. Is everything all right?"

The concern in his voice made it sound even sexier flowing straight into her bloodstream. He had a direct yet caressing way of speaking that made her want to rub up against him with intimate confessions. He already knew she masturbated to his music, it couldn't get more personal than that... and yet it could, it could get much more dangerously personal... "Yes, everything's all right," she forced herself to say.

"Then why don't I believe you? Why is it you can't model for a while, Miranda?"

Oh God! She closed her eyes, desperately willing herself not to tell him, to hold back. "Because..."

"Because?"

"Because of marks left by a leather belt..."

"Mm... Do they hurt?"

"They sting a little, but it's not bad..." She couldn't believe she had just said that.

"No, it isn't, and I think you enjoy being reminded of the pain and the place it took you inside."

"Yes…"

"What were you being punished for?"

"How did-"

"Answer my question, Miranda."

Her breath caught, and she deliberately closed her eyes pretending not to see what she was doing. "I was being punished," she excited herself by drawing out her response, "for lying to my boyfriend."

"And what did you lie to him about?"

"I can't tell you that…"

"Yes, you can. You even want to."

"Richard, I can't…"

"Tell me."

"I fucked another man… and now I'm having this conversation with you…"

"Yes, you're a bad girl, and what's more, you *want* to be bad so you can be punished for it."

"No! I'll never lie to him again."

"And you shouldn't lie to him, but do you really believe that means you'll never fuck another man again?"

"What?"

"Is this man your Master?"

"I don't know… I don't call him that, but *yes*, he is, he's the master of my heart and soul. I love him more than anything."

"Then he's the one I should be talking to."

"What?" she repeated, almost laughing. The conversation had taken such a wild turn she almost felt safe because she was no longer obliged to take it seriously.

"Those are the rules, Miranda. You'll learn."

"I have to go now, Richard…"

"I want you to tell your Master about me. I want you to give him my card and explain that I want you to pose for me again in private, and in varying degrees of bondage. Tell him I'll pay you two-hundred dollars an hour, and that I'll want you for at least five hours."

"A *thousand* dollars?"

"You heard me. I'll expect an answer soon. If your lovely marks fade, I'll have to give you new ones."

This time she did laugh. "You're crazy!" she exclaimed, to dead air; he had already hung up, insultingly confident she would do exactly as he said.

Chapter Twenty

Sarah had just finished testing her insulin levels when the phone rang. Her caller ID told her what she couldn't believe – it was Miranda on a Friday night. She picked up, curiosity getting the better of her resentment.

"Well, hello there, my long-lost friend."

"Sarah, I'm sorry, I've been wanting to call you."

"Forget it, I understand, you're in love; nothing else matters."

"It *does* matter. I'm sorry."

Her voice softened sincerely. "It's okay." She would do the same in Miranda's shoes. They should have been ruby red slippers or glass high-heels but instead they were black leather boots.

"I need you, Sarah."

"Trouble in paradise?" she quipped, despising herself for it but unable to resist.

"If you only knew…"

Sarah perched on the edge of her seat. She had never heard quite that tone of voice from Miranda before – enigmatically husky and languid as if she had just come, and yet worried, too. "If only I *knew…?*" she prompted.

"I can't talk about it on the phone. There's a lot you don't know, Sarah, and I'm pretty sure a lot more is going to happen whether I want it to or not. I think I do, but I just don't know how it possibly can…"

"Whoa! What are you talking about, girl friend?"

"Can you come over?"

"Now?"

"I just put a vegetable lasagna in the oven…"

Sarah glanced in the direction of her kitchen and its nearly empty cupboards. She was a take-out junkie, not exactly good for her diabetes, but a girl had to get her pleasures somewhere. "Vegetable lasagna?" she echoed longingly.

"Please come over, Sarah."

"Okay. I'll call a cab and be over soon as I can."

"Thank you!"

"This better be good."

* * *

At least I can afford a cab, Sarah thought glumly, slumping in the back-seat of the anonymous vehicle. The truth was she could use a healthy and filling vegetable lasagna. She missed Miranda's cooking, and resented that a man was now being given all the culinary treats once reserved for her. But that was the fate of all sidekicks everywhere, to be shoved off the stage once the real reason for the drama got going – the torrid romance between the lead man and woman. So here she was, sitting invisibly in the dark wings of a taxi getting ready to walk out under the lights again and react appropriately, mouthing comforting lines in response to Miranda's intense confessions, whatever they might be. Just for once she would love to break free of the script and really give the girl a piece of her mind. Yet she could never bring herself to be as scathing with her as she had no problem being with everyone else.

The divine smell of baking cheese greeted her out in the hallway and made everything feel worthwhile. She knocked briskly, inhaling blissfully. She couldn't remember the last time she'd enjoyed a home-cooked meal.

Miranda opened the door and exclaimed, "Sarah!"

Only then did Sarah remember the change she had made to her appearance since she last saw her best friend. She pushed past her and sashayed into the apartment, exaggerating the sway of her hips clad in tight blue London jeans from *Victoria's Secret,* her ass enticingly defined beneath a brown leather Bomber jacket. She turned on her boot heels like a model, and patted the full wave of freshly dyed blond hair framing her face in a modern retro style evocative of Dietrich and Monroe.

Miranda had closed the door and was grinning at her. "You look *fabulous!*"

"Thank you, *darling.*" She shrugged off her jacket and hung it up. "It was time for a change. The nineteen-twenties were great, but I need to catch up to the new millennium."

"You look beautiful as a blonde, Sarah." Miranda reached up and stroked her soft hair. "It really brings out your eyes… they look so big and so brown…"

Sarah took a step back. "Yeah, like chocolate," she scoffed. Miranda had never touched her like that before and it felt strange… nice. "So, where's the wine?"

"Red or Chardonnay?"

"Red, please, a Merlot."

"I'll be right back."

Sarah made herself comfortable on the loveseat. She could see no evidence of Michael anywhere, but then again Miranda was obsessively neat. If he had left a pair of socks, or better yet an underwear, lying around, his girlfriend would have picked it up, washed it and folded it neatly for him.

Miranda returned and offered her a brimming glass. "Here."

"Aren't you drinking?"

"I've already had half a bottle of Chardonnay and two ibuprofens."

Sarah sat up alertly, but took a long swallow of wine before asking, "Okay, what's up?"

* * *

Two hours later, Sarah was still struggling to control the resentment, jealousy and concern building inside her like storm clouds occasionally releasing flashes of sarcasm that made Miranda's eyes burn indignantly for an instant even though they were powerless to truly affect her. Sarah had realized on Christmas Eve that her friend had a kinky streak, but for some reason she had believed Michael was more conventional. She never even bothered to imagine he would relish giving Miranda everything she wanted, and more. She should have known better. One of Miranda's greatest virtues was how absolutely honest she was, and how bravely she dared to express her deepest, darkest thoughts. She should have known her sweet friend would be even more open with Michael, her purported soul mate, and like a good Lady in Waiting, she, Sarah, should have anticipated all the dangers her trusting princess was headed for. Her princess was deep in the woods now, covered with red slashes as she ran around in circles, not knowing if she truly wished to find a way out of her increasingly kinky predicaments or not. And to make matters worse, or even better, a darkly handsome villain was thickening the plot. It had always amused Sarah that people didn't realize just how violent fairytales are.

"My God," she whispered, reverently caressing one of the marks left by Michael's belt. "This must *seriously* have hurt."

"It did."

Sarah frowned at the hint of pride in Miranda's voice. Her beautiful friend was living in another world, a world of perfect health where she could willingly let her lover inflict whatever he desired on her flesh because she knew it would bounce right back and quickly heal into flawless perfection again. It was a world Sarah could scarcely comprehend, condemned as she was to electronic monitors and insulin needles and the countless pills that soothed her aches and pains and crippling migraines. It seemed a travesty, a sin, that someone so blessed with beauty and health could wish to sink into the quagmire of pain others had to struggle to climb out of every day. But, of course, she knew it was not the same, and that it was jealousy (not to mention her orthodox upbringing) making her think this way. She had to clear her head; she couldn't help Miranda if all she had to offer was blind indignation.

They were sprawled back across the loveseat now, their legs stretched out in front of them. Sarah's belly was so pleasantly full of lasagna she had unzipped her jeans, and the wine was both mellowing her out and inspiring her to speak her mind. "You've stepped into a whole other world, Miranda."

"Tell me something I don't know."

"But you *don't* know, that's the point. You don't realize this world functions under a completely different set of laws than the ones you're used to and are still expecting."

"What do you mean?" Miranda turned her head towards her on the cushion and fixed her with an intent stare that wrested the words out of Sarah before she even knew what she was thinking.

"What was it Richard said to you on the phone, *you'll learn?* He said a hell of a lot to you in those two words, Miranda."

"Learn *what?*" she demanded.

"That conventional laws of love don't work in this world, and what's more, they're not even the laws you really want to live by. You love Michael, you want to be with him for the rest of your life, I don't question that, I don't doubt the special bond between you if you both feel it. I'm even willing to believe he's your precious soul mate, but the point is, you still fantasize about fucking other men. You *want* to fuck other men, Miranda."

"But why do I want that if I truly love Michael?" She turned her head away again and stared up at the ceiling like a lost saint failing to see the heavenly host materializing. "Which I do, I love him more than anything."

"That's another mistake you're making, and you're in good company, most everyone makes this same mistake and it leads to infidelity and unhappiness all around. The mistake is to believe that love and sex are inextricably bound together, when in reality they often don't have anything to do with each other. You fucked Patrick on Christmas Eve and yet it didn't change how much you love Michael, did it?"

"No."

"I rest my case."

"But that's *not* the point because I can't ever do it again. I can't ever lie to Michael again!"

Sarah sat up impatiently. "I need some more wine." She reached for the bottle and killed it in her glass. "You are so obtuse sometimes, Miranda. Richard told you he didn't expect you to lie to Michael, didn't he?"

"Yes..."

"Answer me this. What was Michael so upset about? Why did he punish you tonight? Because you fucked another man, or because you didn't tell him, because you lied to him by keeping it from him? That first night when you asked him to spank you, you told me he said it turned him on what a bad girl you were. Are you getting the picture now?"

"Are you actually telling me Michael wouldn't mind if I fucked Richard if he knew about it? Right! You're crazy, Sarah!" All her virtuous hackles were up. "That's like saying I wouldn't mind if he was fucking another girl right now as long as I knew about it!"

Sarah stood up and paced the room as she talked fast. "Obviously that's not what I'm saying, I'm talking about things you just might possibly enjoy doing together. Your outraged values are blinding you to subtleties, Miranda. How can you be so blindly certain it wouldn't turn Michael on to watch you fucking another man if he gave you permission to, if he *commanded* you to do it? You say he's not the jealous type. He knows how much you love him, and he seems more than willing to use your body for his pleasure in ways most men would never dream of, so why not imagine it might also turn him on to watch another cock sliding in and out of you? Being an artist, it might excite him to watch you getting fucked from all sorts of different angles."

"Sarah!"

"He can't fill all your holes at once, can he?" She went on relentlessly, enjoying the wicked nature of the serious sermon she was delivering. "Oh sure, he can use sex toys on you, but it wouldn't be the same. I think he'd probably get off fucking your pussy while another man fucked your mouth, or vice versa. Why not? And don't tell me you wouldn't love it, too, if that other man was sexy, especially if you found him irresistible like you do Richard. It seems to me that you and Michael would both benefit from spending some time with this guy. He sounds like he could probably teach you a lot. It's obvious from his music he's experienced in the lifestyle. He could help clear away the moral cobwebs you keep getting tangled up in and needlessly terrifying yourself with. This is a whole new reality, and if you have no idea what you're doing, you and Michael are going to end up causing each other a lot of unnecessary pain and grief. You need to expand the rules of your relationship, the parameters of so-called true love, but you can't, not until you stop being afraid."

"Sarah!" Miranda sighed. "I love you!"

"I love you, too." She was more moved by the passionate declaration than she revealed. "And you have to be open to the possibility that it might actually turn *you* on to watch Michael fucking another girl."

"Never!"

"God, now I understand why he beats you sometimes! You can be so stubbornly selfish, Miranda. Think about it. Is that really how you feel or is it how you *think* you should feel? If you're really soul mates, if you really trust in your love for each other, you're also completely free to do whatever you both please together, whatever feels right, and obviously being one-hundred percent monogamous doesn't feel right to *you*, if it did, you wouldn't be having sexy phone conversations with masterful rock stars or fucking married men in basements!"

"Are you calling me a hypocrite, Sarah?"

"If the shoe fits, Cinderella. Be careful, don't let the controlling indoctrination of church and state limit and skew you're thinking. You've reached the point where you can either shatter your enviably exciting life around yourself or live happily ever after in a world where, like a real prince and princess, you and Michael live by your own rules and to hell with what everyone else thinks. Did you really expect that just meeting your soul mate was the answer to all your problems? Even true love isn't easy, Miranda."

Chapter Twenty-One

Thirteen Months Later

Miranda was walking down her street listening to *Sieve's* new CD on her ipod, a proud smile on her lips. She was almost home, but *her* song had only just begun, so she slowed down. It was a brisk May evening. She was wearing form-fitting black cotton leggings with matching socks and sneakers, and a hip-length black lack leather jacket revealing a band of color provided by the clinging violet shirt she had on beneath it. Michael had commented more than once on how delicious her ass looked in this outfit, thrust invitingly up and out as she walked with her back naturally straight and proud. Her posture had always been excellent, but hours spent posing in varying degrees of bondage had mysteriously heightened her confident (Richard called it her *regal*) carriage. Not even standing motionless for hours posing for "normal" art students had made her so conscious of all her movements.

It was twilight, her favorite hour, another reason to linger outside for a while. She came to a complete stop on the sidewalk, her vision focused inward on the lyrics playing in her head and flowing through her blood straight down into her sex. It was still thrillingly hard to believe this song had been written for her, *about* her, and that she had experienced all its sexy – many would say shocking – images. She was surrounded by apartment buildings yet she was standing alone on the street… one of the blinding flashes of sunlight reflected on western facing windows had transported her into another world where anything is possible, a world where all her desires could come true if she was brave enough to believe they could, and that they should.

She perched on the curb, preparing to cross the street after the car moving slowly towards her passed. She could easily have run, even walked, in front of it, but the song was coming to a climax and she was transfixed by it. The electric sound of Richard's screams as he climaxed in the musical scene he had painted never failed to ignite her responsively wet pussy with a shock of desire that made her catch her breath as the music pulsed violently inside her, ascending to a brutal crescendo that left her feeling weak and longing for more in the sudden silence afterwards.

She pulled her earphones out, inevitably reminded of how more than once two cocks had slipped out of her at the same time. The memory of their synchronized driving rhythms never failed to make her feel weak in the knees, and for this reason she remained standing on the curve even after the white car drove by. She was lost in a memory so hot, she didn't see the cop until he was standing right in front of her.

"Miranda Covington?"

"Yes?" she gasped. The flashing lights took her completely by surprise – electric blue serpents slithering over the white cruiser throwing the synapses in her brain into a confused panic.

He grasped one of her arms. "Come with me, please."

She was so surprised she stumbled off the curb, and he steadied her by tightening his grip on her. "Why, what did I do?" she asked.

He didn't answer, he simply opened one of the cruiser's back doors, obviously expecting her to slip meekly inside.

"Let go of me!" She panicked and wrenched her arm out of his grasp. "You haven't even told me why you're arresting me!"

As swiftly as a magician performing a magic act, he slipped a pair of handcuffs on her wrists, securing her hands in front of her. "Watch your step," he said, resting a warm hand on her head and gently but inexorably forcing her into the car.

Miranda was so stunned she didn't say anything as he casually closed the door behind her. He slipped into the front passenger seat because there was another police officer sitting behind the wheel. She was no stranger to being handcuffed, but it had never been real before, not like this, and her heart was beating so hard she almost couldn't hear herself think.

The car began moving down the street again, leaving her apartment building behind, and a rush of fear made her demand with aggressive bravado, "What's going on here? Why are you arresting me? I haven't done anything!"

"Yes, you have," the cop behind the wheel replied firmly, "you're dating my son."

"You're Michael's father!?" She was so relieved she sank back against the uncomfortable seat, yet the protective grill separating her from the two men in front was humiliating. Her tumultuous feelings felt like caged animals breaking all civilized laws, which made her next words sound ridiculously incongruous even to her. "It's a pleasure to meet you, sir."

The cop on the passenger side chuckled, and glanced over his shoulder at her. "She's sweet." His warm, dark-brown eyes made his teeth look strikingly white as he grinned.

"Be quiet, Miguel."

"Yes, *sir*." He laughed again.

"Michael misses you," she declared because it was true.

"Does he."

"Yes." She looked down at the heavy handcuffs on her wrists feeling like a complete virgin to bondage simply because the vital key of her safe word was missing.

"You're going to break up with him."

"What?" She stared at the back of his close-cropped blonde head. "You can't be serious?"

"I am." He glanced at her. "And you will."

The hard lines of his face stunned her as she glimpsed the ghost of her young lover in them, only Michael's jaw was strong without being obstinately square, his nose was more elegantly defined, and his eyes… there was nothing about this man's eyes that remotely reminded her of his son's beautifully penetrating stare.

"*No*, I won't!" She defied him fiercely. "I *love* him!"

"Did you love Pat, too?"

As though he had literally struck her, she suddenly felt strangely dizzy and couldn't think, much less speak.

"You're not good enough for my son." He moved in for the kill when she remained silent. "You're easy, Miranda." He went right for her throat. "He's enjoying himself with you now, and I don't blame him, but you're not the kind of girl he wants to marry and have kids with. It's bad enough he's wasting his time in art school, but he'll come to his senses eventually. Law enforcement's in his blood whether he realizes it yet or not, and when he does, he's gonna want a nice girl who'll be a loving and *faithful* wife to him, not a girl who takes all her clothes off every day for money."

She realized a quiet dignity was her only defense against the vicious moral beating she was getting. "I'm an artist's model, not a whore."

"So you're saying you've never fucked any of your clients?"

"Mike…"

"Shut-up, Miguel. Answer my question, young lady. Have you ever fucked any of the guy's who've paid you to strip naked for them? If you have, that makes you a slut in my eyes."

"Okay, that's enough, Mike. You said you were just going to have a little talk with her, not ream her."

"It's okay, *Miguel*,", she savored his name gratefully, "he can't help it if he's an ignorant hypocrite."

Mike's partner sucked in his breath, but there was a glint of respect in his dark eyes as he glanced back at her again.

"Michael knows you've cheated on his mom more than once," she went on sweetly, "so why is a faithful wife so important to a cop, exactly? So you can get off breaking all the laws of love while she looks the other way all meek and mild? And if I fuck a client, it's not for the money. He's paying me to pose for him, not to fuck him, I do that for free if I like him, and I never do it behind Michael's back, he's always there with me. Sometimes it turns him on to watch, and to share me, and other times it really excites me to watch him with another girl. It's a real turn on feeling what he feels and seeing what he sees and helping him fuck her."

"*Dios mio!*" Miguel breathed. "And you want her to break up with your son *why?*"

"Because she's white trash! Listen to her!"

"I'm listening, believe me."

"Let me out of here!" she demanded. "You have no right to restrain me like this. It's not a crime being in love with your son and making him happy in every possible way, which I do, and which I always will! You're the one who's hurting him by cutting him off the way you have! Let me out of here!"

He turned the steering wheel all the way to the right so abruptly she was flung across the seat, and then she couldn't regain her balance as the car bounced hard over a curve, dangerously accelerating into what she could immediately tell was a parking garage – the screeching of the tires echoed sinisterly, and it grew so dark in the squad car all her courage was extinguished like a candle beneath this gust of rage.

"You okay back there?" Miguel asked.

"Yes," she reassured him, very grateful for his sympathetic presence as she sat up. "But I want to go home... please." Her voice broke.

"Mike, what the fuck are you doing, man?"

He parked, shut off the engine, and got out.

Miguel immediately followed him, but Mike had already flung open her door and pulled her out of the car. He was wearing a black uniform of course, and he was a tall, powerfully built man with broad shoulders and lean hips just like his son, only he was older; his body was fuller and stronger, and even more impossible to resist as he made her face a wall. He had parked in the very back of the garage, in a dark corner almost completely hidden by a broad concrete beam. He grabbed a fistful of her hair at the back of her neck, and pressed her cheek hard against the cold concrete.

"You need to learn some respect, young lady," he said quietly.

"Let go of her, Mike…"

Her eyes closed beneath a blinding rush of fear because suddenly Miguel didn't sound so sure about the position he wanted to take here.

"You're going to help me teach her a lesson, Miguel." Still painfully clutching her hair, he turned her to face his young partner, and forced her down on her knees.

She was surrounded by darkness – the cold shadows at the back of the garage and the slick cloth of two black uniforms still cool to the touch despite the warm, hard male bodies inside them, their hips weighed down by dangerous weapons that terrified her even as they helplessly turned her on… she felt herself falling into an all too familiar trance as her body reacted to the situation with a submissiveness languidness that was mysteriously deeper and stronger than the outrage being broadcast by her brain…

"See how easy she is?" Mike said. "Come on, partner, she *wants* to suck your big Cuban cock. She says she loves my son, but she'll let both of us come in her mouth if we want to, like a good little slut."

"No!" she whimpered, yet she didn't close her eyes, she was too entranced by the sight of the young cop's hands reaching for his belt as if he really meant to open his pants…

Miguel sank to one knee in front of her and quickly snapped the handcuffs off her.

As if the sound triggered something inside him, Mike let go of her hair abruptly and stepped back.

She quickly got to her feet.

"Your son would never have forgiven you, Mike," Miguel said, "and I really don't think that's what you want." The expression on his face – hard with anger and yet also somehow tender from the depth of understanding in his dark eyes – made him look strikingly handsome to Miranda.

"I won't say anything," she promised.

"She'll have to walk from here." Mike spoke as if she was no longer there.

"I think that's best," Miguel agreed neutrally, but he caressed one of her cheeks before turning away. He slammed the door closed behind him as the police car backed up, burning rubber again on its way out of the garage.

Miranda shivered and passionately hugged herself. She was suddenly trembling so violently she couldn't even think of walking until her knees solidified. She anxiously patted the pockets of her jacket. She was still intact – her wallet and her ipod and her keys were safe. She was all right, nothing really bad had happened. It didn't matter that this wasn't true; she had to believe it was until she was safe inside her apartment. Only then could she allow herself to remember those moments she had spent on her knees in a dark corner of a parking garage with two cops in full uniform pinning her between them…

Oh God! She started walking as fast as she could, eager to escape the concrete chill that made her even more shamefully aware of the hot excitement that stabbed her and, unbelievably, began bleeding a profound regret that the experience ended just before it crossed a seriously forbidden edge. She could not *possibly* be disappointed she hadn't sucked Michael's father's cock or the intriguingly foreign dick of his handsome young partner. She could not *possibly* have enjoyed being so coldly used and humiliated, it was only exciting in retrospect because she was safe, because she was still pure and intact and on her way home. Yet, in a way, she dreaded going home now even more than her helplessness a few minutes ago in the hands of two strong and commanding men, because it was entirely up to her, and no one else, whether or not she told her lover about what his father had said, and almost done, to her.

Chapter Twenty-Two

Miranda told Michael what had happened the minute he got home. They were living together now in her apartment, and even though her landlady had raised the rent somewhat, they were both still saving money. Financial considerations had nothing to do with their decision, however. After six months, it simply felt ridiculous to be separated by a bus and a train ride when they wanted to be together all the time.

She poured him a glass of wine and gave him a few minutes to relax before she dropped the bomb quietly and calmly, sheltering him from the worst of it by not telling him exactly what his father had said about her. She had no desire to call herself a whore even if she was only repeating someone else's opinion. "He said he didn't want me to keep seeing you, that I wasn't the kind of girl you would want to marry and have kids with. Of course I told him I had no intention of breaking up with you because I love you."

He set his wine glass down and grasped both her hands. "I'm sorry, Miranda, he had no right to do that."

"It's okay, Michael." It saddened and disturbed her that she couldn't bring herself to tell him the whole truth – that his father had called her a little slut, and that she had almost behaved like one on her knees in a dark parking garage pinned between two cops. She left Miguel out of it completely. There was no point in mentioning her sensual curiosity about his big Cuban cock...

"No, it's not okay." He dropped her hands and stood up angrily.

"I think he really misses you, Michael."

"And kidnapping my girl friend and insulting her is how he shows it?"

"I know it seems strange, but some people have a hard time expressing their emotions and-"

"Stop trying to defend him." He loomed over her where she sat perched on the edge of the loveseat. "Are you telling me everything?"

Whenever she sat with her back straight, her hands clenched in her lap, it was a dead give away she was not feeling relaxed, and what made her tense more than anything, they both knew, was not telling him the whole truth about something.

He sank to his knees and cupped both her clenched hands in his, soothing the tension out of her fingers by gently caressing them with his thumbs. "Is that all that happened, Miranda?"

"He called me a slut," she whispered.

"Look at me."

She obeyed him, and the glowing depth of feeling in his eyes washed over her soul like a cosmic wave, dissolving her tense loneliness; making her feel part of all life and the universe holding and loving her as his pupils did. "And I called him an ignorant hypocrite."

He smiled. "That's my girl."

"And that's not all I told him... he made me angry."

"I'm glad you were angry, you had every right to be. It's much better than part of you feeling hurt and worried that what he said might be true… you know, the way you felt after we first… did certain things."

It *had* been hard for her to get used to the fact that sexual monogamy and true love did not necessarily go hand-in-hand. When she and Michael were sharing intense, and technically forbidden, pleasures together, it was easy not to think about it, but during those first months after Sarah opened her eyes and her mind, whenever she was by herself, her self-esteem suffered fevers of shame and fear it took all his patient understanding to nurse her through. "I'm just hurt, Michael, it's not nice hearing things like that about yourself, but I'm not worried…" She just couldn't stop seeing herself on her knees between two black uniforms.

"There's something you're not telling me, Miranda." He grasped her hands and squeezed them hard. "You keep looking away. You're thinking about something, and you need to tell me what it is."

She sighed. "I can't keep anything from you, can I?"

"No, you can't. I don't know why you even bother trying anymore."

She looked straight into his eyes. "Because I don't quite know how to say it… I guess part of me *is* still worried, I mean…"

"Don't look away, Miranda, just tell me what you're thinking."

"Certain things affect me, Michael, and I have no control over it… it doesn't matter what I'm thinking… you know how I feel about strong handsome men dressed all in black…"

"I'm well acquainted with all your fetishes, yes." His voice was both understanding and firm. "What I want to know now is everything that happened to you today."

"Your dad was with another officer named Miguel who tried to defend me, but Mike got angry and drove into a parking garage… he pulled me out of the car and said I needed to be taught some respect." She looked down at their joined hands, unable to continue holding his eyes as she told him the rest. "He said they were going to teach me a lesson, and he forced me down onto my knees in front of his partner... ouch, Michael, you're hurting me."

"I'm sorry." He let go of her hands. "Go on." It was a command.

"And that's when it happened, *nothing*. I didn't do anything. I think I said 'no' but I didn't try to get away, it doesn't matter that I knew I couldn't because Mike was grabbing my hair so hard it hurt, I still didn't really try to stop what was happening, I just said 'no', one silly little 'no' that sounded more like 'yes, please' even to me. Your dad said I was easy. He said, 'See how easy she is, Miguel? She *wants* to suck your big Cuban cock'. I think maybe that's when I said 'no', I don't remember, all I clearly remember is how I felt... even though I was angry and scared and I didn't actually want it to happen, part of me was turned on, I couldn't help it... their black uniforms and their weapons and how hard your... your dad was holding me, and then Miguel looked like he was going to open his pants and I didn't say anything, nothing! But instead he knelt down and snapped the handcuffs off me. He said, "Your son would never forgive you for this, Mike, and I don't think that's what you want' and they let me go."

Michael straightened up slowly. "You neglected to mention the fact that they'd handcuffed you, Miranda."

"I'm sorry..."

"Yes. Who cuffed you, and when?"

"Miguel did before he put me in the car."

He picked up his wine glass and sat down on the ottoman across from her. "Is that everything?"

"It's enough, don't you think?" His cool tone riled her. "You're thinking your dad's right, aren't you? You're having second thoughts about us suddenly, admit it! You're thinking I *am* easy and you can't possibly even think of marrying me. You're just having fun with me a for a while just like your dad said you were!"

He drained his glass, set it carefully down on the rug beside him, and then placed both hands on his knees, his back straight. "Are you quite finished?"

She felt sick at heart, as though she'd just thrown up the poison she was forced to swallow that afternoon in a police car. "Yes." She gripped the cushions on either side of her to keep from clenching her hands in her lap again.

"I'm not going to punish you for insulting me, and yourself," he began quietly, "because this time it's not your fault. You suffered a very unpleasant experience today, and I'm truly sorry about that. You're *not* easy, Miranda, but it *was* too easy for them to make you doubt yourself and put a profound dent in your self esteem. Your belief in yourself and in me and in *us* has to be a lot more resilient than that, yet you made the best of a bad situation. I think part of you felt safe enough to be turned on because the man threatening you was my father and he is, in a very real sense, a part of me. Deep down you knew that no matter what they did to you they wouldn't actually hurt you."

She stared down at the rug as she asked softly, "But what if they'd actually made me suck their cocks?"

"But they didn't."

"No, but part of me was ready to… it's like I couldn't resist the whole scene…"

"I know, but what you have to understand is that I love that part of you, too, I love everything about you. You're sensually submissive to handsome, dominant men, especially when they're in full uniform. I've known this about you for a very long time, Miranda, it's part of the beautiful mystery of who you are, and it in no way – as you very well know, I hope – affects how much I respect you. Your being the way you are is also part of who I am, a handsome dominant man, and if you didn't respond to me the way you do, I could never be completely fulfilled and as happy as I am with you."

"But I *love* you, Michael, you're much more than just-"

"I know, Miranda, and I love you. That's why I'm your Master. Even though you don't call me that, you know that's what I am, don't you?"

"Yes…"

"And as your Master, I'm here both to protect you and to give you what you want because that's what *I* want, and that's what turns *me* on. What happened to you today wasn't right, but you did nothing wrong, my father's the one who crossed a line he shouldn't have crossed, and he realized that, because in the end he let you go."

"But any normal girl wouldn't… wouldn't have almost regretted the fact that they let me go…"

"One of the reasons I love you so much, Miranda, is *because* you're not a normal girl, thank God. You've had nothing but good experiences with your submissiveness, you're accustomed to indulging this part of yourself because you've always done it safely with me. Like I said, even though he was being a bastard, you were still with my dad, and even though he was a stranger to you he's also a part of me, and you knew this deep down and were letting yourself go the way you're used to doing with me. You were overwhelmed, but instead of shutting down in fear, your courage and your profound self-esteem took the mysterious form of excitement. I hope you're never faced with a situation like that again, but I'm proud of the way you handled yourself. You didn't behave like a helpless victim. Your beautiful submissiveness gives you a very real power over men that was abused this afternoon, but you're hardly to blame for that."

She raised her eyes from the rug and stared at him in wonder. "You're the most beautiful man on earth, Michael. Every time I think I've come to a dark dead end inside myself, you reach into my feelings and open a door onto a much more complex world than I could ever have dreamed of!"

He stood up. "Come here and suck my cock, baby." He unzipped his jeans. "Just close your eyes and pretend it's that big Cuban dick you were deprived of today."

Chapter Twenty-Three

Five Months Later

Even before they were living together, whenever a heating oil delivery was scheduled, Michael was sure to be there to sign for it. Miranda had not seen Patrick since that afternoon in the basement, although she had often heard his voice from where she sat in the living room. Michael always stepped out into the hallway but left the front door open a crack behind him, as if to let Pat know she was inside and could hear whatever they said. The first few times were decidedly tense, then a month or so after Michael moved in, the whole torrid affair suddenly seemed to be forgotten, as if intense and passionate feelings come with a mysterious expiration date after which they harmlessly evaporate.

Roughly five months after Miranda "met" Michael's father, there was a brisk knock at the door. Michael wasn't home (he had an evening class that semester) and it was Miranda who opened the door wearing her favorite black robe. The sight of Patrick standing on the threshold was so unexpected, it rendered her speechless for a long moment like a physical blow.

"Is Michael home?" he asked shortly, not bothering to conceal the fact that he had intended to catch her alone.

She was tempted to lie and say, "Yes, he's in the shower" but there was no sound of running water to back her up, and the blood was rushing through her body so fast coherent thoughts were temporarily swept away by her pounding pulse. "No, he's in class." She had learned the hard way that telling the truth was always best even if it was also the most dangerous thing to do.

"Good, because I'd like to talk to you." His hands were thrust into the pockets of the black leather coat she remembered all too well; he wasn't hiding behind an official clipboard tonight.

"Really, talk to me about what?" she heard herself ask innocently.

"May I come in?" There was a glint of anger in his eyes that told her he didn't appreciate having to ask.

"I don't think that would be a good idea, Patrick. You lied. You promised you wouldn't tell anyone about us, and yet you told Michael's dad, of all people. I can't tell you how much I appreciate that, thank you."

"He's my best friend, Miranda, and I had to talk to someone."

"And I don't suppose talking to your wife was an option, huh?"

His eyes narrowed. "You lied, too, Miranda. You told Michael."

"Oh yes, that's true." She scarcely recognized the sweetly sarcastic voice emanating from her. She had never spoken to any one like this before in her life, yet she couldn't seem to stop herself, and how good it felt to taunt him made her realize how much his last words to her, and the tone in which they were spoken, had been festering inside her, *You stand naked in front of com-*

plete strangers for money. "Well, then, I guess we're even, Patrick. Good night." She began closing the door.

He shoved it open, pushing her back into the apartment as he stepped inside, just as she had known he would; just as some devilish part of her had deliberately goaded and tempted him to do. Yet instead of sobering her up, his violent gesture made her feel even more intoxicatingly out of control. "You know, I could have you arrested for this, Patrick." She tightened the sash of her robe to make sure it wouldn't fall open, and yet also to draw attention to the fact that she was naked beneath it like on that night that completely changed her life. "I think I'll call the police." She walked towards the phone, but then spun around again to face him, feigning mock surprise. "Oh, but I forgot, your best friend's a cop, and he thinks I'm a slut who's not good enough for his son. Michael deserves a nice *faithful* baby machine like his mother and like your wife. I hear they're the best of friends."

He slammed the door closed behind him, strode over to her, and slapped her gently. "Stop it, Miranda, I came to apologize!"

She caressed her cheek, grateful he had been man enough to kill the sarcastic hysteria she couldn't seem to control even though it was making her hate herself. "It's your wife you should be apologizing to."

"That's none of your concern. I came to tell *you* I'm sorry I warned Michael to stay away from you because you'd hurt him. I should never had said that, but I was jealous; I wasn't thinking straight. I should never have told his father who you were, but like I said, I was angry. I told myself I was concerned for Michael, but that was bullshit. The truth is I wanted to see you again, and the attitude his dad took towards you, the ugly things he said, made me realize I really didn't feel that way about you at all. I just lost my head for a while, and I'm sorry."

"It's okay, Patrick, I'm sorry, too. I didn't mean to speak to you like that just now, I guess I was more hurt than I realized thinking you had such a low opinion of me after we… you know."

"I know, and I've felt like shit about it all this time, but I couldn't bring myself to ask Michael for permission to talk to you."

"Has it really been almost two years?"

"Yes…"

"That's a long time to feel bad about something, and the last thing I want is for you to feel bad, Patrick."

"That's not how I felt when I was fucking you."

"No, that was nice…"

"Nice?"

"It was fantastic!"

They were standing like mirror images of each other, hands thrust deep into the pockets of their respective black garments, their eyes locked.

He lowered his voice. "Is it true Michael shares you with other men sometimes, Miranda?"

"Oh my God," she took a step back, "his dad told you that?"

"That's what he said *you* told him."

She quickly moved past him. "Patrick, you shouldn't be here." She slipped a hand out of her robe and rested it significantly on the doorknob. "Michael will be home any minute," she lied. His class would go on for another hour and then he had the long commute home, but there was always the off chance he would decide to skip his class, and she had no intention of being caught alone with another man.

He turned to face her, but remained were he was. "I'll go, Miranda, as soon as you answer my question."

"I'm not obliged to answer any of your questions," she pointed out reasonably; desperately.

"I think you just did."

She opened the front door a crack. The cooler air out in the corridor felt good, but it didn't help clear her head of the jumble of hot thoughts, possibilities and dreads his presence stirred up inside her. "You wouldn't understand, Patrick. It's not how you make it sound."

"How do I make it sound?" he insisted quietly.

"It beats cheating on each other in private," she snapped. "When I want a man, I tell him, but that's only happened once, and I'm sure it won't happen very often at all. It's not something we do every weekend, you know, it's not like that at all. It rarely happens…"

His hands remained deep in his pockets, as if he didn't want to frighten her by revealing them. "And when he finds another girl attractive he tells *you?*"

"He finds lots of girls attractive, if he didn't he'd be dead," she retorted, "just like I find lots of men attractive, but that doesn't mean I actually want to fuck them all. We've been together almost two years now, and we've only been with another man once, and with another girl just once. It felt right at the time, but it's not something we make a habit of."

"You don't need to sound so defensive, Miranda, I'm not judging you."

"So many marriages don't work out because couples can't be honest with each other like this." She couldn't stop herself. She had given this a lot of thought and mentally lectured herself like this more than once.

"It seems like a dangerous game to play if you're really in love with someone."

"Cheating on your spouse and lying to them is a dangerous game, too."

He moved closer to her. "You have a point."

His sudden surrender wiped whatever remained of her impassioned speech out of her mind as she dared to look him straight in the eye. "You've heard the expression *where angels fear to tread*, Patrick. I can't really say anymore than I have..."

He was standing so close to her now all he had to do was stretch his arm out to close the door.

She didn't mean to whisper. "What are you doing?"

"I just have one more question to ask you before I go."

She remembered now how arresting his clear gaze could be as he ran the ball of his right thumb across her mouth, gently pressing it into the furrow formed by her lips.

"Do you still want me, Miranda?"

The end of his slightly rough thumb was resting on her bottom lip, she couldn't open her mouth to respond without being afraid she would end up sucking on it if she did. She didn't want to because even this small act would be a betrayal of her lover's trust, and yet of course she *did* want to, and he knew it. She turned, quickly opened the door again, and stepped out into the chilly corridor. "I think you know I do," she finally replied from the relative safety of a public place. It didn't matter that there was not another soul in sight; technically, they weren't alone in her apartment. If Michael came home the scene would not be as incriminating; she would not be betraying his trust.

He followed her out. "So, what can we do about that, Miranda?" He slipped an arm around her waist and pulled her to him.

"Pat-"

He kissed her, not roughly as he once had, but slowly, lingeringly, savoring the flavor of her tongue wrapping around his.

She channeled all her fear and indignation into the kiss so that she seemed to be passionately responding to him, and in a very real sense she was, there was no denying it. She waited a little too long to plant her hands against his cold black leather chest and push him away. "Patrick, I love

Michael!" she gasped. "I love him much more than I can ever desire another man. Don't you understand? If you want me so much, you have to talk to him."

Now he was the one who took a step back in disbelief, which gave her the chance to slip back into her apartment.

She gazed out at him sadly. "That's the only way it can ever happen again, Patrick."

"Well, call me strange, but it just wouldn't be the same." He pulled the keys to his truck out as if to make the point that he wasn't turned on anymore.

"Why, because it wouldn't be forbidden and dangerous?" she taunted. "Have you ever fucked a girl with another man before, Patrick? You wouldn't believe how tight it makes her."

His eyes were strangely blank as he stared at her, his body half turned away from her, ready to walk away and yet not moving.

"Please don't be mad at me, Pat," she said urgently. "You have to understand I'll never again do anything behind Michael's back. It doesn't mean I'm not seriously tempted to, but you asked me what we could do about it, and I told you... goodbye." She made herself close the door and lock it before pressing herself back against it. Her heartbeats sped up waiting for the sound of his heavy boots walking down the corridor. It wasn't that she was afraid of not being able to resist letting him back in if he insisted; her resolve to always be true to Michael was profoundly unshaken. Her heart was racing because the longer he stood out on the landing, the more excited she became by the possibility that he was actually considering what she had said. At last she heard him leaving, and she suffered a stab of grief knowing she would never see him again.

She sighed, both deeply disappointed and relieved as she walked over to the window and looked down at the street. She heard the sound of the truck's engine revving up and felt it in her womb where she was sure he would never be again. And she was okay with that, it didn't really matter; all that truly mattered was now much she loved Michael and how much he loved her. And in a way, Patrick was right – the forbidden brevity of their encounters *did* have a lot to do with how exciting they had been and how good his cock had felt precisely because it wasn't supposed to be inside her. Yet she had learned from experience it was a cheap and disappointingly short-lived thrill fucking someone behind someone else's back. It was much more arousing, and the pleasure was deeper and lasted much longer, if you fucked someone right in front of someone else, *with* them.

Chapter Twenty-Four

"**M**y dad called me today."

"What?" Miranda turned to Michael from the stove where she was stirring a big pot of turkey chili. "When?" She quickly set the wooden spoon down, and sat across from him at the table.

"While you were in the shower this morning."

"Why didn't you tell me?"

"I'm telling you now."

"What did he say?"

He shrugged. "Not much." He finished his beer.

"He must have said *something*," she insisted gently.

"My mom probably made him call."

"It's about time he listened to her!"

"She knows how happy we are together." He stood up and got another beer out of the refrigerator. "She knows I plan to marry you." He sat down again, leaning comfortably back in the chair as he opened the bottle with his bare hand.

She stared at him.

"He feels bad about what he did and wanted me to apologize to you."

"Then I hope you told him I was sorry for calling him an ignorant hypocrite." She did not pursue his casual mention of marriage, but she secretly savored it like the finest wine – a mystical vintage bottled the day she was born at last ready to be opened and shared with the right man who could appreciate everything as deeply and passionately as she did.

"You can apologize to him yourself when we go over there for dinner on Christmas Eve."

"He invited us to dinner on Christmas Eve?!"

"No, my mom did, but at least he didn't forbid it."

"Oh Michael, I'm so glad! You see, I *told* you he missed you."

"Hmm. When will they be here?" He changed the subject.

"I told them seven. They should be here soon."

Right on cue, there was a knock at the door.

"Her date's very punctual," he observed; by herself, Sarah was always at least half-an-hour late.

Michael made himself comfortable in the living room while she answered the door.

Sarah was standing out on the landing, alone. "Hi, sweetie!" she cooed happily. "Let me in, I'm freezing!" she added stridently.

"But where's your date?"

"Finding a parking spot." She began divesting herself of gloves, scarves and hat.

Miranda glanced down the corridor, curious to meet the new man in her friend's life.

"Hey, beautiful." Michael helped Sarah slip out of her coat, and then hung it up for her along with the rest of her soft winter armor.

"*Hola*, Michael!" Bracing herself on his broad shoulders, she reached up and kissed him on the cheek. "*Como estas?*"

"*Muy bien, gracias, y tu?*"

"*Soy fantastica!* I'm brushing up on my Spanish."

Miranda grinned, her attention torn between Sarah's radiant face and the dim hallway as she remained holding the door hospitably open. "Sarah, you look so happy."

"I *am*, and you'll know why when you see him. But he's not just gorgeous, he's unbelievably sweet, and smart, too. I met him in my new Gnostic Gospels class!"

"Really?" Miranda frowned, listening intently, because she thought she heard someone banging on the front door of the building.

"Oh my God!" Sarah shrieked. "I forgot he doesn't have a key! I'm so used to just letting myself in with the copy you gave me-"

"It's okay," she said soothingly. "I'll run down and let him in, you just relax."

"I have a glass of your favorite Merlot waiting for you, Sarah."

Miranda heard Michael luring their guest into the living room as she ran down the hall and raced down the steps, going round and round and yelling, "Just a minute!" when she reached the first floor. Breathlessly, she pulled open the heavy door, and then stood behind it to protect herself from the cold as the person waiting outside quickly stepped inside rubbing his black gloved hands together briskly as a frigid gust of wind chased him in. His back was to her; all she saw was a tall figure with short dark hair over a black leather jacket as she hurriedly closed the door behind him.

"Thanks!" he said with feeling.

"Sorry." She smiled, turning to face him. "Sarah forgot... Miguel?"

"Miranda?" His eyes obviously still adjusting to the dim light, he stepped closer to her in an effort to see her better.

"It's me," she said faintly as those heady moments on her knees in a dark parking garage suddenly came crashing back.

"*You're* Sarah's best friend?"

"Yes, but don't hold it against her, Miguel. She really likes you, and you don't need to worry, she's not like me…"

He laughed, then abruptly cupped her face in his cold gloved hands. "I won't tell her if you don't…"

"There's nothing to tell," she protested with absolutely no conviction.

"Yes," he whispered, letting her lips feel the warmth of his breath, "unfortunately." He released her, smiling softly, but his eyes were impenetrably dark looking her slowly up and down as she moved past him towards the stairs.

She was sure Michael would guess right away this was the same Miguel who had handcuffed her; the same Miguel who was his dad's partner and supposedly possessed of a big Cuban cock she had wondered about more than once since that afternoon when she was forced onto her knees before him, and then watched him going for his belt as if he really meant to open his pants, but instead he reached for the key that freed her.

"I'd say this was a hell of a coincidence," he remarked as he followed her up the steps, "except I don't believe in coincidence."

"I don't either!" she agreed. He was walking so closely behind her she could feel the cold exuded by his leather jacket mingled with the tantalizing warmth of his body inside it. "I call it the Magic Pattern," she told him, recalling where Sarah had said she met him.

He laughed again. "Yeah, I like that, the *Magic Pattern*… "

Before they reached the second landing, she turned abruptly to face him. She had the advantage of being a step above him, yet that only put them face-to-face. "I told Sarah about what happened that day, Miguel," she warned him. "We can't hide it from her forever that it was you…"

"I have no intention of hiding anything from her," he replied firmly even as a teasing smile never left his lips. "It's not as if you actually sucked my cock, Miranda."

"No, but I wanted to," she confessed softly, without meaning to, but she couldn't resist; she didn't even try.

He took the final step so he was looking down at her again. "Did you, *really*?" His eyes looked impossibly dark in the dim light of the stairwell.

"Yes…"

"Well, I think Sarah will be flattered to know," his voice dropped to an insinuating murmur again, "how much you once wanted to suck her boyfriend's cock…"

"That's *true*…" His seductive reasoning seriously pleased her, so much so that she forced herself to start up the steps ahead of him again.

"I'm more worried about how Michael will feel about it," he added.

"Oh don't worry about him, he understands."

"*Ay*, Miranda!" There was nothing sarcastic or demeaning about the deep sound of his laughter; it was open and honest and literally made her feel warm all over as its subtle vibration traveled up her spine. "I very much like your *Magic Pattern*, *bella*. I'm ready for some magic in my life, aren't you?"

"Yes, Miguel," she smiled at him over her shoulder, "I always am!"

* * *

Miranda watched Michael's face. She could never get enough of his smooth skin and the strong yet refined elegance of his features which had made his father's face look so blunt and crude by comparison.

She didn't need an excuse to gaze at him worshipfully. From the beginning, she had seen him as a young god taken human form just for her, and very often his profound understanding of her thoughts and feelings *was* a bit uncanny. Of course she knew he was only human, but that didn't make him any less special in her eyes, on the contrary – it was amazing that a real man could be so well rounded, so sensitive and intelligent and considerate and yet also absolutely masterful and completely unapologetic about his dominance. She loved gazing at his face, and tonight she was studying it intently. She could see in his eyes that he was in the mood for some serious fun, and even though he hadn't said anything, she sensed she wasn't the only one in the room aware of an exciting undercurrent being stirred up by the silent yet irresistible energy of his desires. She responded to the subtle clues of his body language by getting up out of her chair and sinking to her knees at his feet, her half full glass of wine cupped in her hands like a chalice. She smiled dreamily at the other couple as he stroked her hair, letting her know he approved of her action and that much more was to come and was expected of her. She glanced up at his face, mainly because she loved seeing it from every possible angle, each one seeming to reveal different aspects of his personality. He was staring over at Sarah, who was going on and on about something even though no one was really listening (and perhaps sensing this made her nervous and even more verbose than normal) a dangerously soft smile on his lips and a glint in his eyes that filled her with a very real sense of awe, as if she was seeing two distant stars reflected in his irises promising other worlds where anything was possible if you dared to go there.

Miguel laughed. "I don't know what possessed me!" he declared when Sarah finally stopped talking.

Miranda turned her head. The sound of the young Cuban man's laughter was at once intoxicatingly relaxing and stimulating combined with four glasses of wine.

"I walk into the classroom," he went on, "already seriously regretting it, when suddenly I see this beautiful girl sitting there and I thought, there really *is* a God."

"Oh stop it!" Sarah punched his arm. "I'm *not* beautiful."

"Yes, you are," Michael said quietly.

Sarah blushed to the roots of her blonde hair. Miranda could almost forget it was dyed admiring the way it framed her big brown eyes with such naturally soft luminosity, and her cheekbones had become strikingly visible after she lost twenty pounds when her doctor insisted she improve her diet and start exercising. She glanced up at Michael again, a hot green tendril of jealousy suddenly uncoiling in her chest and interfering with her breathing.

He met her eyes, and the smile vanished from his lips as he leaned forward and kissed her, tilting her face up towards his by grasping the hair at the back of her head, firmly but not painfully as his father had done. Yet she knew he was deliberately reminding her, and everyone else, of that afternoon as he tongued her deeply, his passionate kiss telling her how much it turned him on to be watched as he possessed her, and that if he had anything to say about it this was only the beginning.

She allowed herself to be swept along on the deepening current of his lust wondering how Miguel and Sarah were reacting. Were they staring at them in shock or were they becoming inspired and kissing as well? They were perfectly silent, yet she thought she heard a soft rustle of cloth that made her imagine they had moved closer together and were embracing. When Michael at last released her, sitting up again, she glanced up at him first to brace herself before looking over at the loveseat.

Miguel was sitting on the edge of the cushion with his legs spread and

Sarah was kneeling between them with her back to him, her eyes fixed on Michael as her date's hands slowly reached down and caressed her breasts through the white silk blouse.

"Put down your glass, Miranda," Michael commanded her quietly.

She obeyed him, supporting herself on one arm as she reached over to set her unfinished wine on a table.

"Mm…" He spanked her as she unconsciously offered him her ass. He didn't need to say it for her to know he wanted her to kneel between his legs with her back to him so that she and Sarah were facing each other across the room. She couldn't look up at his face anymore, she could only feel his hands caressing her along with the even more exciting pressure of his willpower forcing her to let go of any tense doubts and fears she had about what was happening.

Sarah's eyes met hers for a split second, and literally at the speed of light Miranda knew exactly what she was feeling. She had been aware from the beginning that Sarah was helplessly attracted to Michael, she often jokingly remarked she couldn't blame Miranda for doing whatever he said, and now she was getting what she had not so secretly wanted for a long time – Michael's divided yet intimate attention, his appreciation touching her in every way except physically, although under the circumstances she could easily imagine those were his hands unbuttoning her shirt. And meanwhile Miranda gladly suffered the same fate as Miguel's dark eyes fixed on her doubled the exciting impact of her lover's caresses. She wasn't wearing a blouse that could be slowly and seductively opened, so she obligingly lifted her arms and Michael pulled the shirt off over her head, exposing her breasts in one swift motion. Sarah moaned, and her eyes closed as Miguel impatiently snapped open her bra, a sexy front closure model from *Victoria's Secret*. He cupped her full tits in his hands even as his eyes devoured

Miranda's pert bosom, and the suggestive way he licked his lips made her nipples harden as if she could actually feel his tongue licking them.

Whatever Michael did the other man reflected with his actions like a dangerously enchanted mirror, and vice versa, until it was unclear who was directing the action as they all became dancers obeying an irresistibly powerful erotic choreography. The only person Miranda touched was Michael, yet while she fervently sucked him down she also seemed at last to be savoring Miguel's big Cuban cock, her mouth and her eyes wide open as she watched his erection disappear and reappear between Sarah's straining lips. She was enthralled not just by the size of his dick, which was no more impressive than Michael's, but by how different his skin was – a smooth, enigmatically opaque golden-brown with no hot blue veins pulsing beneath its fine surface alerting her to when he was close to coming, almost as if he could fuck a girl all night without ever growing soft... her imagination ran wild and her lips and tongue and throat responded accordingly, so much so that Michael let go of her head, further inspiring her with the knowledge that she was doing such a good job of pleasing him there was no need for him to direct her. He reached down and fondle her breasts then spanked her ass, making her moan around him. Sarah was in the same position she was – naked on her hands and knees – Miguel's strong fingers threaded possessively through her hair as he strictly controlled the motion of her head, his swift, rhythmic strokes occasionally slowing down as his head savored the arduous caress of her throat. Like Michael, he had pulled off his shirt and shoved his jeans and underpants just far enough down his thighs to free his cock. No matter how long she blew him, Miranda couldn't get her fill of Michael's hard-on as she stared over at Miguel's firmly defined pecs and six-pack abs. She had never seen such an unyielding stomach on a man, and it violently turned her on to match the motion of his hips with her bobbing head as she literally felt his pleasure growing and mingling with her lover's in a way that was almost palpable in the quiet room, in which Sarah's slurping devotion to his erection sounded obscenely loud. At first Miranda wondered if she was doing something wrong because she made hardly any noise at all when she went down on a man, but then she proudly stuck to her own style because it was obvious she was greatly pleasing Michael with it. She had suffered the same momentary insecurity about her small breasts when Miguel exposed Sarah's heavier bosom, until she experienced the electrifying certainty that how different their tits were made them absolutely perfect as Miguel caressed softer, fleshier globes staring at the dramatically long hard nipples jutting from provocatively pert mounds caressed by Michael as he in turn stared at bigger and softer offerings.

By the end of the night, Miranda felt wonderfully sated, as if she had fucked both men even though only Michael had touched her. Miguel came in Sarah's mouth, not hers, she tasted only her beloved boyfriend's sperm, yet she wasn't suffering from any unfulfilled fantasies; everything was absolutely right with the universe as she drifted off to sleep in her future husband's arms.

Chapter Twenty-Five

Along but easy walk to her favorite grocery store, *Trader Joe's*, helped make up for the ludicrous fact that Arlington was a dry county. She had to go all the way to Cambridge for her wine. When she lived alone and couldn't afford a cab, that was quite a chore, but life was so much easier now that she lived with Michael. They went wine shopping every month and took a cab home together. Daily life had never felt so effortlessly enjoyable.

Miranda took her time strolling down the isles planning the week's menu while scanning the shelves for new and exciting items. Michael loved her cooking, but she was nowhere near satisfied with her culinary skills. She still depended entirely too much on cook books; only recently had she become intuitive and confident enough to come up with her own recipes by combining different herbs and spices however felt right, daring to risk a muddled result. So far, most of her tentative experiments had paid off. Michael possessed an incredibly discerning palate, and he did not hesitate to tell her when he felt there was too much or too little of a particular ingredient, and sometimes he even suggested one or two she never would have thought of. His sense of smell was much more acute than hers, which undoubtedly had something to do with the discerning sharpness of his taste buds. Whatever the explanation, he never failed to impress her. He seemed to know a great deal about everything. Even though he was useless in the kitchen, he was familiar with techniques used by gourmet chefs, and was able to list all the ingredients of classic dishes as well as more exotic ones she had never heard of. And the same was true about their sex life. Shortly after they met, he began making a thorough study of BDSM, and he occasionally described practices to her that made her cringe. He had no intention of applying them to their life, but his desire to understand how everything worked in scientific detail made him read up on a subject until all sources available to him at the time were exhausted, and only then was he comfortable with his understanding of it. She was grateful for his thoroughness, and the longer she knew him, the more she loved and trusted him, and the safer she felt obeying his commands.

She invariably spent more money than she meant to when shopping for food, but she could afford to living with Michael. She had a smile on her face as she lifted her two heavy cloth bags and walked out of the store into a freezing December evening. Inevitably, when she passed it on her way home she looked towards the old church on the opposite side of the street in front of which, a few weeks ago, she had seen a tall and handsome priest. He was dressed all in black; this was the detail that caught her attention, his physique did the rest. His body wasn't concealed beneath a shapeless cassock; he was wearing black slacks and a black top that was half suit jacket, half coat, but whatever it was, it showed off his broad shoulders. His blonde hair was shaved close to his skull and glimmered like gold beneath the streetlight that flickered to life as she studied him. She turned off her ipod and stood staring at him on that particular evening. She was on her way to the grocery store, but she suddenly changed her mind and impulsively crossed the street. The priest was talking with two teenage girls who were hanging on his every word. She couldn't blame them; this man of God possessed a presence that drew her towards him like a black magnet. There was no way he was gay; she could read the lines of a man's body and tell if he was straight, although the real test came when she met his eyes. She wanted to speak to him herself even though she had no idea what the hell she would say, but it was the only way she could get his attention so she had to think of something. He was standing in front of a Catholic church, which naturally meant he was a Catholic priest, and her blood was silently singing a strangely sweet hymn as she approached him as though she was walking back into her innocent past. When she was a little girl she went to confession every month, which struck her as ridiculous now because at the time she had no idea what sin was. It was a very different story lately. In the eyes of official church doctrine, Miranda Covington had sinned countless times, and the list of her transgressions had multiplied seven-fold since she met Michael, her beloved soul mate.

She ran in front of two cars on her way to the other sidewalk remembering how Sarah had called her a typical Catholic school girl tormented by feelings of guilt that made her crave punishment. Miranda had given the subject a great deal of thought since then and concluded that Sarah was right, in a sense, but it didn't mean that the dark bent of her sexual desires wasn't also much more profoundly complex. She had touched on another facet of her sexual submissiveness in her first e-mail to Michael in which she described some of the things she fantasized about him doing to her. If as a woman her nature embodied the earth, then she *had* to suffer as the earth was suffering now under a brutal patriarchal regime raping her resources and tying her down with the metal shackles of industries pumping her cancerously full of landfills and pollutants, some of which would take centuries to dissipate. There were, she estimated, all sorts of reasons to explain her deep-seated kinkiness, but in the end she really didn't care what they were. All she knew was that when she saw a tall and handsome man dressed all in black who also sported an aura of confidence and authority she was drawn to him like a moth to a flame. A bright light is utterly black on a photographic negative; it was the mysterious force of a true man's willpower she couldn't resist. The fact that this particular man was a priest sworn to chastity made her angry, and that was the main reason, Miranda realized, she was walking towards him almost defiantly. She wanted to glimpse in his eyes when he saw her, even if for only a split second, the awareness of all he was missing as he suffered the sinfully fleeting urge to break his vows with her. She wanted her beauty to tempt him and to taunt him with the choice he had made to sacrifice his sexuality, which in ancient times was as valid a path to spiritual enlightenment as any, before the official Catholic Church replaced erotically charged gods and goddesses with one supreme, and highly intolerant, asexual Being.

The setting sun's dying light was suddenly reflected in the stained glass windows behind the priest, forcing her to squint to protect her vision from the bloody halo crowning his military buzz cut.

"Thanks, Father," she heard one of the girls say respectfully as they both began walking away.

She paused, waiting until he was completely alone to approach him, but he suddenly turned and started briskly up the steps; in a moment he would disappear into the church.

"Father!" she called, but a truck was rumbling down the street and he didn't hear her. She hesitated a moment, then ran after him, taking the steps two at a time even though she still had no idea what she was planning to say to him. "Father?" she repeated breathlessly.

He turned at the sound of her voice, his hand already gripping the large black wrought iron handle set in the heavy wooden door. His expression was sobering in its indifferent neutrality before a smile curled his lips that did not reach his eyes. "Hello," he said, and waited.

"Are you new here, Father?"

"No, actually, I've been here for years." His eyes narrowed slightly, and she imagined he was thinking that since she obviously wasn't one of his parishioners she didn't merit that much of his time and attention. He surprised her by offering her his hand. "I'm Father Devine."

She almost said "You're kidding!" but stopped herself just in time; the last thing she wanted was to tritely repeat what he must have heard a million times. "Pleased to meet you, Father." She dared to hold his eyes as her skin rested against his during a tantalizingly brief but stimulatingly firm handshake. "My name's Miranda."

"Hello, Miranda." His smile deepened curiously, almost, but not quite, illuminating his clear blue eyes. "What can I do for you?"

"Do you take confession, Father?" she blurted, unable to come up with anything else.

"Yes… I do," he replied carefully, his eyes assessing her and forming conclusions she couldn't even begin to read. "On Saturday afternoons between one and five."

"Oh… okay."

He hesitated, and then seemed to force himself to add, "Unless you really feel the need to unburden yourself now…"

"Oh, no, I'll come back on Saturday, thank you!"

"Are you sure?" She won his full attention. "It's no trouble."

"It would take a long time, Father. I have a lot to confess. I'm not saying

I regret any of it, but…" She looked down at the centuries-old stone floor.

"It's okay." He walked up to her, and rested a hand lightly on her shoulder. "I won't judge you, Miranda."

It pleased her that she had to look up at his face, and especially that he had touched her. She loved tall, handsome men… tall, handsome men with big hard cocks… "I'm just curious to know what you'd say, Father. I can imagine what you'd think, but I'm hoping maybe I'm wrong, that once I explain how I feel about it you might understand…" His eyes were gazing with polite attentiveness into hers, but his blue irises felt disappointingly shallow. "Because the fact is, a few *Our Father's* and *Hail Mary's* would not be nearly enough penance," she concluded.

He wasn't touching her anymore but he didn't back away as he asked, "So if you're not sorry for what you've done, and you're so sure you know what I'm going to say about it, why do you want to go to confession, Miranda? Is it *about* the penance? Are you feeling guilty about something you've done and looking for someone you believe has God's authority to punish you for it?"

She smiled to conceal a dark spark of excitement at the thought of him truly punishing her. "No Father, I told you, I don't feel guilty. I saw you standing here and for some reason… I don't know… I just had to talk to you, I'm sorry."

"That's what I'm here for, Miranda, there's no need for you to be sorry."

"Yes there is because, to be perfectly honest, I thought you were intensely handsome, and that's no reason to talk to a priest."

"I'm flattered." This time when he smiled his eyes actually shone with indulgent amusement… and some other emotion she couldn't define much as she tried. "However, I get the feeling that's not the only reason you're here, Miranda. I'd be happy to take your confession whenever you feel like sharing all your dreadful secrets with me."

She laughed, entranced by the unexpected mischievous glimmer in his eyes. They would have looked striking above his tall, black-clad body if it wasn't for the stiff white collar digging into his throat in a way that looked much more uncomfortable than any bondage she ever endured at Michael's loving hands. The sight sobered her up. "No Father," she said gravely, "that would be disrespectful of me because, you see, my motives aren't pure. I'm not looking for absolution, I'm…" She glanced at the ponderous facade of the church behind him. "I'm selfishly looking for excitement by wanting to tell you everything just to see how you'll react, and that's wrong, that *is* something I'd be ashamed to do."

"I think I understand." His tone was neutral. "But just remember I'm here if you need to talk, Miranda. You shouldn't over analyze your desire to confide in a priest. It sounds like you're reaching for excuses not to do something you'd find difficult and yet that a part of you clearly feels the need for."

She gazed up at his face amazed he hadn't understood her at all, or maybe he had and this was his way of deflecting her attraction to him since it was a hopeless dead end. "Thank you, Father, I'll remember." She turned away and switched on her ipod, occupying herself searching for *Sieve's* latest CD as she felt the man in the impotent black suit staring after her. Richard had behaved more like a priest with her than Father Devine ever could. Nevertheless, when she got home she wrote a poem about him.

FATHER DEVINE

Watching him walk across the courtyard all in black
on a sunny Sunday morning, sitting on the grass
dressing the dirt waiting for my laundry to dry,
his stride was so swift and sure it quickened
my pulse until I saw the white collar

around his throat my desires defy like wild horses a fence.
He was greeting people as they flowed out of church
purified inside, and back in the Laundromat I stared
out at him through the stained glass. Two young men
speaking to him were vague faces across the street,
but he stood before me in vivid telephoto,
his tall black form a mysterious light meter,
the world coming into meaningful focus
around the inviolate center of his faith.
Then he disappeared into the church, and out in nature
I felt uncontrollably moody as the weather, my heart
a seed aching with the need to feel myself
all of a man's desires. Nuns are rootless flowers
in chastity's glass fading on lifeless altars,
never blooming to their fullest in soft beds.
Yet the soil of faith is the only thing that's real
in the universe of his black suit, his heart a star
burning through all doubts to the iron core
of certainty in the life-giving power of love's
eternal energy… Amen… A man!

THE POWER OF WORDS
To capture your feelings
handcuff them in vowels,
bar them behind consonants,
sentence them to blank pages,
and watch them break free
on the wings of an open book.

Chapter Twenty-Six

When Michael got home from his night class, Miranda knew at once something was wrong. She helped him off with his backpack and then hugged him, deliberately pressing her naked breasts into his cold leather jacket and shivering from the thrilling contrast between her warm sensual skin and the frigid temperatures outside still clinging to him. He was also still wearing his gloves, and she loved the cruelly possessive way they gripped her ass. Tonight, however, there was no real energy in his embrace, and disengaging herself from him, she looked curiously up at his face.

"You're coming down with something," she observed.

"I'm fine," he said listlessly, shrugging off his jacket and leaving it on the floor instead of hanging it up as he usually did. His gloves met the same fate. "You look beautiful," he added belatedly. She had braved the chill of their apartment and greeted him completely naked except for a black pair of extreme high-heels.

"Thanks!" She smiled wryly, a bit disturbed not to see the slightest spark of desire in his eyes. "What can I get you to drink?"

"Just some ice water, thanks."

Now she knew he wasn't feeling well.

The next day he skipped his classes and Miranda called in sick herself so she could stay home and nurse him. That was her excuse, but the truth was she didn't have the energy for the long commute with her better half lying at home on the couch. He was snuggly clad in his robe and a pair of socks only because she asked him, very sweetly, as a favor to her, to try and stay as warm as possible. She discovered that dominant men did not make very good patients; she could not insist he do anything, she could only suggest, and very casually, so that it seemed entirely like his decision and something he felt like doing not something he *had* to do. She entertained herself making home-made chicken soup, and she didn't need to offer him a second bowl because he always loved her cooking and it had nothing to do with the fact that he was sick. She indulged his moods feeling as if she was nursing a wounded lion, which deepened her admiration for him, but by the end of the day her nerves were feeling frayed.

She fed him dinner – a big juicy Buffalo burger and oven fries, one of his favorite meals – and afterwards she managed to get him to drink a cup of hot Peppermint tea. They cuddled on the loveseat watching TV and went to bed early. Miranda wasn't sleepy, but she wanted to tuck him in, and then press her naked body against his before he drifted off, after which she read by the light of her bedside lamp for over an hour trying not to feel anxious. It was flu season, everyone had a cold these days, yet she had known Michael for two years now and she couldn't remember him ever being sick. Her boyfriend succumbing to a seasonal cold was no reason for her to be feeling so strangely on edge.

She put the book aside and made an effort to analyze her emotions... exposed and inexplicably disappointed... they made absolutely no sense. Her boyfriend had the flu, big deal, it wasn't cancer or anything seriously life threatening, God forbid. But she couldn't help it, she felt disproportionately sad and afraid. This was the first time she had faced the thought of losing him; the first time she had seen him looking and feeling in the slightest bit vulnerable. His immune system was fighting a virus invisible to the naked eye and there was nothing sexy about the conflict or the strength he had to exercise to win back his good health. If he got really sick he wouldn't be able to protect her or command her to do things, he wouldn't even have the energy to desire her, much less fuck her. The Michael she knew would be mysteriously mummified by tissues and blankets as their dynamic sex life was temporarily buried.

She turned off the light, disgusted with herself. Michael caught a simple cold and suddenly awareness of his mortality came crashing down around her. Her feelings were completely over the top sometimes; all the time. She knew he was in perfect health, he would kick this bug in no time, a lot more easily than she'd get over how unbelievably selfish she was being. Dredging to the very bottom of her reaction to his indisposition, Miranda acknowledged that she resented being confronted by his mortality and all the weaknesses inherent within it. In her eyes, he wasn't just a man – he was living proof of the Magic Pattern, he was the dynamic daily fulfillment of all she could possibly want as in his hands her body and soul bloomed as they never could alone. But he was also just another human being, a mind and heart separate from hers, and it was this fact that made their love for each other so miraculous.

She turned and pressed herself against his back in the darkness, tenderly spooning him, confident she wouldn't wake him; he slept as deeply as a baby.

"*My* baby," she whispered, "my man and my Master, my love and my life!" He was much more precious to her resting trustingly naked in her arms than he could ever be wearing black leather boots and pants and gloves – the priestly vestments that turned her on so much when he used them to revere the mystery they embodied in this world and, she passionately hoped, forever in endless others.

About the Author

Maria Isabel Pita is the critically acclaimed author of over ten Erotic Romances, two Non-Fiction Erotic Memoirs and a collection of Erotic Stories set all through history. For a description of her books, and more, please visit www.mariaisabelpita.com

pamphlets and broadsides the English reading public were offered in the 19th century. It can only be hoped that this Anthology may stimulate the reader into further adventures in erotica and its manifest reading pleasure. In this unique anthology, 'erotica' is a comprehensive term for bawdy, obscene, salacious, pornographic and ribald works including, indeed featuring, humour and satire that employ sexual elements. Flagellation and sadomasochism are recurring themes. They are activities whose effect can be shocking, but whose occurrence pervades our selections, most often in the context of love and affection. This anthology includes selections from such Anonymous classics as *A Weekend Visit*, *The Modern Eveline*, *Misfortunes of Mary*, *My Secret Life*, *The Man With A Maid*, *The Life of Fanny Hill*, *The Mournings of a Courtesan*, *The Romance of Lust*, *Pauline*, *Forbidden Fruit* and *Venus School-Mistress*.

The Collector's Edition of Victorian Lesbian Erotica
Edited By Major LaCaritilie

Fiction/Erotica · ISBN 0-9755331-9-3
Trade Paperback · 5 3/16 x 8 · 608 Pages · $17.95 ($24.95Canada)

The Victorian era offers an untapped wellspring of lesbian erotica. Indeed, Victorian erotica writers treated lesbians and bisexual women with voracious curiosity and tender affection. As far as written treasuries of vice and perversion go, the Victorian era has no equal. These stories delve into the world of the aristocrat and the streetwalker, the seasoned seductress and the innocent naïf.

Represented in this anthology are a variety of genres, from romantic fiction to faux journalism and travelogue, as well as styles and tones resembling everything from steamy page-turners to scholarly exposition. What all these works share, however, is the sense of fun, mischief and sexiness that characterized Victorian lesbian erotica.

The lesbian erotica of the Victorian era defies stereotype and offers rich portraits of a sexuality driven underground by repressive mores. As Oscar Wilde claimed, the only way to get rid of temptation is to yield to it.

The Collector's Edition of the Lost Erotic Novels
Edited by Major LaCaritilie

Fiction/Erotica · ISBN 0-97553317-7 ·
Trade Paperback 5-3/16"x 8"· 608 Pages · $16.95 ($22.95 Canada)

MISFORTUNES OF MARY – Anonymous,1860's: An innocent young woman who still believes in the kindness of strangers unwittingly signs her life away to a gentleman who makes demands upon her she never would have dreamed possible.

WHITE STAINS – Anaïs Nin & Friends, 1940's: Sensual stories penned by Anaïs and some of her friends that were commissioned by a wealthy buyer for $1.00 a page. These classics of pornography are not included in her two famous collections, *Delta of Venus* and *Little Birds*.

INNOCENCE – Harriet Daimler, 1950's: A lovely young bed-ridden woman would appear to be helpless and at the mercy of all around her, and indeed, they all take advantage of her in shocking ways, but who's to say she isn't the one secretly dominating them?

THE INSTRUMENTS OF THE PASSION – Anonymous, 1960's: A beautiful young woman discovers that there is much more to life in a monastery than anyone imagines as she endures increasingly intense rituals of flagellation devotedly visited upon her by the sadistic brothers.

The Story of M – A Memoir
by Maria Isabel Pita

Non-Fiction/Erotica · ISBN 0-9726339-5-2
Trade Paperback · 5 3/16 x 8 · 239 Pages · $14.95 ($18.95 Canada)

The true, vividly detailed and profoundly erotic account of a beautiful, intelligent woman's first year of training as a slave to the man of her dreams.

Maria Isabel Pita refuses to fall into any politically correct category. She is not a feminist, and yet she is fiercely independent. She is everything but a mindless sex object, yet she is willingly, and happily, a masterful man's love slave. M is erotically submissive and yet also profoundly secure in herself, and she wrote this account of her ascent into submission for all the women out there who might be confused and frightened by their own contradictory desires just as she was.

M is the true highly erotic account of the author's first profoundly instructive year with the man of her dreams. Her vividly detailed story makes it clear we should never feel guilty about daring to make our deepest, darkest longings come true, and serves as living proof that they do.

Beauty & Submission
by Maria Isabel Pita

Non-Fiction/Erotica · ISBN 0-9755331-1-8
Trade Paperback · 5-3/16" x 8" · 256 Pages $14.95 ($18.95 Canada)

In a desire to tell the truth and dispel negative stereotypes about the life of a sex slave, Maria Isabel Pita wrote *The Story of M... A Memoir*. Her intensely erotic life with the man of her dreams continues now in *Beauty & Submission*, a vividly detailed sexual and philosophical account of her second year of training as a slave to her Master and soul mate. *"A sex slave is very often a woman who dares to admit to herself exactly what she wants. Absolute submission to love requires a mysterious strength of character that is a far cry from the stereotype of sex slaves as mindless doormats with no self-respect. Before I entered the BDSM lifestyle with the man I now call "my Master" as casually as other women say "my husband" I did not believe a sex slave could lead a normal, healthy life. I thought my dreams of true love and my desire for a demanding Master were like matter and anti-matter canceling each other out. I have since learned otherwise, and Beauty & Submission continues the detailed account of my ascent into submission as an intelligent woman with an independent spirit who is now also willingly and happily a masterful man's love slave."* From Beauty & Submission

Cat's Collar - Three Erotic Romances
By Maria Isabel Pita

Fiction/Erotica · ISBN 0-9766510-0-9
Trade Paperback · 5 3/16 x 8 · 608 Pages · $16.95 ($ 20.95 Canada)

Dreams of Anubis: A legal secretary from Boston visiting Egypt explores much more than just tombs and temples in the stimulating arms of Egyptologist Simon Taylor. But at the same time a powerfully erotic priest of Anubis enters her dreams, and then her life one night in the dark heart of Cairo's timeless bazaar. Sir Richard Ashley believes he has lived before and that for centuries he and Mary have longed to find each other again. Mary is torn between two men who both desire to discover the legendary tomb of Imhotep and win the treasure of her heart.
Rituals of Surrender: All her life Maia Wilson has lived near a group of standing stones in the English countryside, but it isn't until an old oak tree hit by lightning collapses across her car one night that she suddenly finds herself the heart of an erotic web spun by three sexy, enigmatic men - modern Druids intent on using Maia for a dark and ancient rite...

Cat's Collar: Interior designer Mira Rosemond finds herself in one attractive successful man's bedroom after the other, but then one beautiful morning a stranger dressed in black leather takes a short cut through her garden and changes the course of her life forever. Mira has never met anyone quite like Phillip, and the more she learns about his mysterious profession - secretly linked to some of Washington's most powerful women - the more frightened and yet excited she becomes as she finds herself falling helplessly, submissively in love.

Praise for Maria Isabel Pita...

Dreams of Anubis is a compellingly erotic tale unveiled in one of the world's most romantic and mystical lands... Ms. Pita brings together both a sensually historic plot and a contemporary Egypt... her elegant style of writing pulls at your senses and allows you to live the moment through her characters. The language flows beautifully, the characters are well drawn, the plot is exciting and always fresh and riveting, and the setting is romantic. I highly recommend Dreams of Anubis for anyone with a love of erotic romance with a touch of magic and mysticism.   Just Erotic Romance Reviews

Maria Isabel Pita is already one of the brightest stars in the erotic romance genre. If you're unfamiliar with her work, she specializes in transporting her readers effortlessly between the past and present, while indestructible true love weaves its eternal spell on her characters' minds and souls.   Marilyn Jaye Lewis

Guilty Pleasures
by Maria Isabel Pita

Fiction/Erotica ISBN 0-9755331-5-0
Trade Paperback · 5 3/16 x 8 · 304 Pages · $16.95 ($21.95 Canada)

Guilty Pleasures explores the passionate willingness of women throughout the ages to offer themselves up to the forces of love. Historical facts are seamlessly woven into intensely graphic sexual encounters beginning with ancient Egypt and journeying down through the centuries to the present and beyond. Beneath the covers of Guilty Pleasures you will find eighteen erotic love stories with a profound feel for the times and places where they occur. An ancient Egyptian princess... a courtesan rising to fame in Athen's Golden Age... a widow in 15th century Florence initiated into a Secret Society... a Transylvanian Count's wicked bride... an innocent nun tempted to sin in 17th century Lisbon... a lovely young woman finding love in the Sultan's harem... and many more are all one eternal woman in *Guilty Pleasures*.

Select Reviews:

'Guilty Pleasures' *is a collection of eighteen erotic short stories. These stories take you on an erotic journey through time, each one taking you further back in time than the story before it, until there is no time at all. Maria Isabel Pita is an imaginative writer with a skill for writing beautiful prose. She has taken her love for history to create a collection of stories that makes you want to keep reading. Her heroines are strong and the tales told from their point of view pull you in and make you want to know more about their individual stories. The author's attention to detail and historical accuracy makes it easier for the reader to fall into the stories as they read. This collection has something for everyone. I would highly recommend this collection of short stories. There is nothing guilty about the pleasure received from reading it.* Romance Divas

Pita does indeed take us through the ages, from the near-future time of 2015 A.D., back through the 20th century, then the 19th, 18th, 17th, 16th, 15th, 12th centuries, back to 1000 B.C., 3000 B.C., through to another solar system, and on to a parallel universe. What will amaze you, if not even alarm you, is Pita's eye for detail and her uncanny feel for the everyday lives of her distant characters. When you read her stories of ancient lovers, for example, you will believe that Pita herself has visited those times and is merely recounting to you first-hand what she observed, endured, and felt while she was there. The storytelling is seamless and flowing. The erotic encounters between her characters are sexually explicit and arousing, sometimes emotionally raw, and often thought-provoking for the reader. Pita's unique imagination is unleashed and she spares no punches. Guilty Pleasures *is an absolute must for any fan of literary erotica.*   Marilyn Jaye Lewis – Erotic Author's Association Review

My Secret Fantasies – Sixty Erotic Love Stories

ISBN: 0-9755331-2-6 · $11.95 U.S. / 16.95 Canada

In *My Secret Fantasies*, sixty different women share the secret of how they made their wildest erotic desires come true. Next time you feel like getting your heart rate up and your blood really flowing, curl up with a cup of tea and *My Secret Fantasies*…

The Ties That Bind
by Vanessa Duriés

Non-Fiction/Erotica · ISBN 0-9766510-1-7
Trade Paperback · 5 3/16 x 8 · 160 Pages · $14.95 ($18.95 Canada)

RE-PRINT OF THE FRENCH BEST-SELLER: The incredible confessions of a thrillingly unconventional woman. From the first page, this chronicle of dominance and submission will keep you gasping with its vivid depicitons of sensual abandon. At the hand of Masters Georges, Patrick, Pierre and others, this submissive seductress experiences pleasures she never knew existed…

"I am not sentimental, yet I love my Master and do not hide the fact. He is everything that is intelligent, charming and strict. Of course, like every self-respecting master, he sometimes appears very demanding, which pains and irritates me when he pushes me to the limits of my moral and physical resistance. My Master is impassioned, and he lives only for his passion: sadomasochism. This philosophy, for it is one, represents in his eyes an ideal way of life, but I am resolutely opposed to that view. One cannot, one must not be a sadomasochist the whole time. The grandeurs and constraints of everyday life do not live happily with fantasies. One must know how to protect one from the other by separating them openly. When the master and the slave live together, they must have the wisdom to alternate the sufferings and the languors, the delights and the torments...."

A Brush With Love
by Maria Isabel Pita

Non-Fiction/Erotica · ISBN 0-9774311-1-8
Trade Paperback · 5 3/16 x 8 · 254 Pages · $12.95

The cobbled streets of Boston wind back into a past full of revolutionary fervor and stretch passionately into the future inside the thoughts and desires of Miranda Covington, a young and beautiful professional artist's model.

Michael Keneen knows exactly what he wants to do in life, even if it means disappointing his parents by not continuing a tradition of three generations in law enforcement. For Michael, artist models are only aesthetic challenges on the path to his Master in Fine Arts, until one freezing December afternoon Miranda Covington takes the stand, then suddenly getting her beauty down on paper isn't all he wants to do.

Lost in hot daydreams that often become reality when she poses for handsome clients in private, Miranda doesn't notice the sea of faces around her while she poses, until Patrick's penetrating blue eyes meet hers. He might not be a cop like his father, but his arresting personality is irresistible, especially when he discovers hidden longings in Miranda that challenge all her conventional ideas about love in ways that excite her like nothing ever has...

Secret Desires:
Two Erotic Romances

ISBN: 0-9766510-7-6 · $12.95

DIGGING UP DESTINY by Frances LaGatta:

Atop Machu Picchu - lost Inca City in the Clouds - archeology professor Blake Sevenson unearths a sealed cave marked by a golden sun god. Behind that stone wall resides a priceless ransom of gold and silver. Hope Burnsmyrehas has a brand new PhD, no field experience, and high hopes. She and Blake clash at every turn, but the chemistry between them makes the jungle feel even hotter.

DREAMS & DESIRES by Laura Muir:

Poet Isabel Taylor buys a stack of magazines for inspiration, and discovers the man of her dreams staring back at her from a glossy full-page electric guitar ad. That night she has a vivid encounter with Alex Goodman in her dreams, and when his band comes to town she joins a crowd of groupies backstage. When he whispers, 'Don't I know you?' the first thrilling note is struck in a romantic tour-de-force in which their desire challenges all rational limits...

MAGIC CARPET BOOKS

Order Form

Name: _____

Address: _____

City: _____

State:_____ Zip:_____

Title	ISBN	Quantity

Send check or money order to:

**Magic Carpet Books
PO Box 473
New Milford, CT 06776**

Postage free in the United States add $2.50 for packages outside the United States

magiccarpetbooks@earthlink.net

**Visit our website at:
www.magic-carpet-books.com**